VENTURA

VENTURA

MONTENEGRO

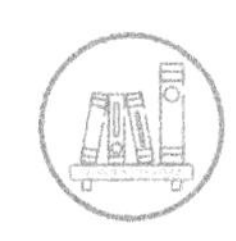

The Creative Writer's Guild at UCR

Este libro es una dedicatoria a mi Abuelito Luis.

This is a work of fiction. The stories, all names, characters, and incidents portrayed in this production are fictitious. Any similarities to actual persons (living or deceased), places, buildings, and products are purely coincidental.

The views and opinions expressed are those of the authors and do not necessarily reflect any official policy or position of The Creative Writer's Guild at UCR, the University of California, Riverside, or the UC Regents.

ISBN 979-8-9879670-3-4

Contents

Prologue

Mist filled the air on a cold winter's night. The town was still, yet creatures remained lurked in the shadows. In spite of that, the night was just like any other. The town had fallen into a deep slumber— the only beings awake were the demons that haunted the dark.

There she waited, blades ready in her hands. Her victim approached slowly as he walked up the alley. She watched his shadow and counted his footsteps. One. Two. Three..... Once inches away, she moved to strike when a voice called out from behind him. She immediately retreated into the shadows before anyone could see her.

The man greeted the person as they mentioned a shortcut that was quicker than the alley. He slowly began walking back. The girl gave a long sigh and returned her blade to its place. She leaned against the wall and pulled her hood forward to cover the rest of her face.

Following the man home hadn't been part of the plan. This would be her third home assassination in two months. The authorities would become suspicious if she killed him there. So it was decided that she would finish him off on the shortcut. If everything went according to plan, she would be able to finish the job, then leave town before morning.

Within one swift movement, she flew up the wall, only touching it briefly before she was over the building. She sniffed the air until she found his scent.

Ventura looked up and in less than a second, she caught sight of him.

Apparently, the shortcut had led into a dark trail through the woods. She smiled. With her luck, she could kill him and make it look like thieves had stolen his riches before the murder. She would get two payments in one night for the price of one job. It was brilliant!

She flew off the roof of the building and dove into trees of the forest where she landed on a branch. Her dark cloak covered her silhouette as he passed beneath her. She felt like a predator stalking her prey, quietly following from branch to branch. She would strike when he was deep enough in the forest for no one to hear his screams.

Murdering her victims in isolation had saved her from troubles in the past. She had done it for so long, it had become part of her slaughter method. Once she disappeared from the scene, authorities were left to wonder who had killed her victim.

Before accepting the job, she had researched her target. His name was Edmund Bellingham, and though he was a lord born from riches, his family had a reputation for being deceitful.

Even before the ripe old age of nine, Edmund had been involved in shady dealings with his father. While at the age of nine those mistakes could have been forgiven, he continued on his path of chicanery and his actions led to much of the poverty within the kingdom. Families lost their land and property to corrupt nobles who were only interested in their own financial gain.

What disgusted her most of all was his lack of compassion for the women and children he had impoverished.

She had dedicated her life to only killing those who lived a life of corruption. Though she was no saint herself, at some point everyone had to face the mistakes of their past. Nevertheless, the true beasts lurked during the day; beasts like Edmund, who contributed to the evils of the world.

When she thought that he was finally deep enough in the woods, she effortlessly slid down the tree. He whirled his head back in fear when he heard her footsteps. She remained hidden in the shadows for her pleasure. Edmund continued walking at a quicker pace than before. His killer smiled. She always did love a chase.

With both blades in her hands, she glided through the trees towards him. When he saw her silhouette flying at him, he started sprinting. Yet even his run was no match for her speed.

As she soared a few feet off the ground, she slashed her sword at his legs, causing him to fall head-first into the dirt. Barely managing to move, Edmund turned around to face her.

"P-please! I'll do better! Please spare me!" He begged for his life, as so many had before him, but she didn't stop walking.

Shaking in terror, Edmund stared up at his attacker. She loomed over him like a dark force with her bloody blade ready. "W-who are you?" he asked with a trembling voice. She raised her head so he could see her turquoise eyes. "I'm exactly what you deserve."

Before Edmund could say anything more, she swung her blade along his neck, making a river of blood flow down his shirt.

As he lay there dying, she quickly went for his rubies and jewels in his pockets, then grabbed him by the collar and pulled his face towards her. Edmund, barely alive, stared at her with helpless eyes.

"You'll be dead soon enough." She followed that statement by cutting his arms and stabbing his side. As more blood oozed, she watched it pour until she decided that it was enough to believe he'd bleed out. She then put her lips on his neck wound and drained the rest.

Once she finished, she released his collar, letting his colorless body hit the ground with a thud as she wiped the little bit of blood she had on her lip. She watched him lay there, his eyes absent of life. Kneeling beside him, she frowned.

"Qué triste. Let's hope you do better in your next life." Using his handkerchief from his coat, she wiped her blade clean before disappearing once again into the night.

Chapter 1

The scene was filthy. The dirt path was covered with blood that had seemed to dry overnight. Edmund's body lay in the middle of the path with a grim expression on his face. The air smelled of death and terror, and by the looks of the road, it was. Omair looked over the body with the royal guards surrounding him. Starting today, the Princess had hired him to oversee Edmund and his affairs, but he couldn't have known that it would be too late.

He gave a long sigh and turned to Aimon, the leader of the royal guard. "Please alert the Princess of what has happened. I will find who did this." He returned his focus to the body.

Aimon awkwardly looked at the other guards. "With all due respect, sir, I think there's no need. It looks like thieves stole his loot."

Omair didn't look up from the body. "You might be right, but as an inspector, I think it's a bit more than that. Edmund was someone of great influence."

Aimon just shrugged. "Whatever you say." He motioned for the guards to leave with him.

They left Omair alone to investigate the body more closely. Carefully, he examined the large wounds. The slashes on Edmund's body were too large to be from daggers, which were typically what thieves used. This meant that whatever was used to kill Edmund was more sizable.

Omair observed Edmund's discolored figure, reaching for his arm where the skin was stiff and dry. He'd been dead for a few hours, then.

Based on how dry the blood was, Omair assumed that Edmund was killed around midnight.

At first glance, it looked like a lot of bloodshed, but Omair had seen enough bodies to know this wasn't nearly enough.

Checking Edmund's clothing revealed other slash marks, but it still wasn't enough to justify the limited amount of blood he saw.

He looked back at the large cuts. He found them amusing. They had clearly been cut with a longsword, but the way the sword was drawn was used more like a katana. Whoever murdered Edmund had been well-trained in the art of swordsmanship. This was from no thief. While his money was gone, the wounds had definitely been from someone who was highly skilled.

Upon further consideration, it seemed odd to Omair why Edmund had been walking alone at night on this path to begin with. Perhaps he was meeting with someone and didn't want to be seen. It seemed to be even more reason why someone would want Edmund dead, if he was sneaking around where he didn't belong.

Omair stood and searched around the body for any other clues. He found a handkerchief that had been wiped with blood. From the angle the sword was cleaned, Omair confirmed that it had been a longsword.

He glanced around for anything that might lead to the culprit, eyes finding footprints that matched most leather boots. The trail led back into town but disappeared after the dirt path ended. Omair smiled to himself.

"Looks like I have a case after all."

****

Sitting at Euryale Tavern, Grant slid a Bloody Booze to Ventura, who caught it in her tanned hand. Her loyal pet Vito lay next to her as he ate the remainder of his kill from the night before. Ventura watched him quietly.

Her plan had been to leave town in the morning, but Talon had caught sight of her and invited her to the tavern, as it had been a few months since she'd been in Verona. She tried listening in on the others' conversations, but was interrupted by Grant. "So, how's assassin life?"

Ventura sat upright and, with her most charismatic smile, said, "Lovely, really. Meals are easy pickings."

The others laughed and raised their booze to her. "To Ventura, the hero who has returned to us once again!" The room cheered, and Vito howled in celebration along with them. Ventura flushed from the unexpected attention.

Grant turned to Ventura, who gave a nervous laugh. "I'm no hero," she tried to protest. She knew that her assassin name Ventura was never associated with heroism— it was more like terrorism.

Grant leaned closer to her. "Course you are; you're the hope this world needs." He patted her hand gently, pulling away at the call of other customers. Grant's words echoed in Ventura's mind as he attended the others' drinks.

She looked down at Vito, who stood on his hind legs to give her a sloppy kiss. "!Ay Vito!" She gave her pet a hug and a kiss on the top of his head to calm him down, and once he relaxed, she looked around at everyone. She remembered coming here when she was young and had no other place to go, not long after deciding to be an assassin. Grant had welcomed her with open arms; had been the first person to accept her since she lost her home, in fact.

Ventura enjoyed being around the monsters there, but knew she would have to leave again soon. She focused on helping towns everywhere, never staying in one place for too long. Whether beast or mortal, she never allowed injustice to rule.

A few days ago, Ventura received a request from the princess of Devontae to assassinate someone from the royal court. She hadn't stated whom, most likely for the concern for the princess's safety, but Ventura had a few members in mind.

Many of the lords and nobles meddled in affairs that should have been left alone, so it was no surprise that the princess was concerned. Though she hadn't given much information about the job, Ventura felt it would be a fairly easy one.

Though she wasn't sure how to bring it up to Grant. She knew he hated it when Ventura left for long periods of time after only being at the tavern for a few hours. Coming back around to her side of the bar, Grant read Ventura's thoughts like they were a page in a book. "Off again, I see." He continued cleaning the glasses from the drinks while keeping his gaze on her, and Ventura finally met his eyes.

"Yeah, I have another job offer in Devontae."

Grant looked away sadly. "I know. I just hate to see you go."

Ventura was about to speak again when the doors of the tavern burst open, quieting the music and the chatter. A tall stranger stepped through in his formal attire. All eyes were on him. He then gave a polite smile to everyone in the room. "Carry on," he said.

While the music started up again and everyone returned to their conversations, the man made his way over to the counter next to Ventura.

Grant looked at him with confusion but shrugged and asked what the man wanted. "I'll take a Spirit, please, sir." Grant nodded and gave Ventura a knowing look. He then turned to grab his drink. Ventura continued drinking her Bloody Booze. The man turned to face her. "You hear anything about the murder last night?"

Ventura remained calm. She had been expecting this moment for a long time; she knew that one day someone would find her. Without missing a beat, she replied, "I don't meddle in the affairs of others." She took another sip of her drink.

He nodded. "I would hope you wouldn't, but it seems you already have." Ventura set her drink down and lowered her head, giving him a threatening look. "You have no idea what I am, do you?"

The man smirked. "You're a criminal, that's what."

Ventura pushed her cloak aside to reveal her swords. "I'm more than that, guerro."

Vito started to growl quietly.

He backed away a bit as he raised his hands in a placating manner. "I don't mean to start any trouble. I just need information." Vito stopped his growling as Ventura turned her back to him. "Listen, I only know it was you there last night, but I need to know who wanted Edmund dead." The man looked down at Vito once more. "I didn't know that you had a dog."

Ventura finally raised her eyes to see him clearly. He was a tall, light-skinned, blond man. This man was definitely privileged and came from high status, based on his clothing—he knew nothing of the life of the villagers.

"First of all, he's not a dog. Second, I don't snitch. Edmund got what was coming to him," Ventura muttered, returning to her glass.

The man was beginning to get impatient with her. He tried to keep his cool in the tavern, but his anger was slowly rising. "I'm sorry, we might have started off on the wrong foot here." He pulled out a bag of coins and set it down on the table for Ventura to see. "I'm sure you know something."

Ventura scoffed. "If you think you can bribe me to sell someone out, then you'd be mistaken. Those who wanted Edmund dead are innocent."

He sighed. "I really didn't want it to get to this, but...." He revealed a small dagger from his coat.

Ventura looked at him as if he was serious. She then revealed her other three swords beneath her cloak. "¿En serio? Really?" She rolled her eyes and turned away from him completely.

The man then snapped. "Alright, listen here-" He grabbed her by the arm, but Ventura already had her sword on his neck.

The tavern went silent. Ventura stood up and pushed the sword deeper into his throat. "I'm no ordinary assassin, so I suggest you go now before you leave this place in a body bag."

He stood frozen in place. He hadn't expected someone so small to be capable of such violence, but his eyes widened as he caught sight of Ventura's fang. "Y-you're a vampire..." he whispered. Ventura paused for a moment before covering her fangs with her lip as she pushed the knife deeper into his throat.

"Get out," she ordered as she shoved him to the ground.

The man stumbled to his feet as Ventura started to walk away from him, but then he blurted, " I've never met a real vampire before...."

Ventura stopped walking and turned to the man, who was walking towards her cautiously.

"I've always wanted to meet one. Please don't send me away! I would love to ask you some questions!"

Ventura shook her head in annoyance. "No, vete ahora. Leave now," she said as she tried to make her way back to her seat, but this man wasn't taking no for an answer.

"No, wait! You don't understand!" He grabbed her arm, then jumped in front of her to prevent her from moving forward. Ventura tried to move her arm away, but his grip was tight. "I'd love to know more about you! Please, give me a moment of your time!" Ventura stared at him in bewilderment. She turned to Grant to see if he could explain his reaction. Grant shrugged once again. Vito even stared at him, befuddled. He stared at Ventura with full sincerity. "Would you honor me the privilege of allowing me to observe you as a vampire?"

Ventura was speechless, but the tavern wasn't. Everyone started to whisper in unison. Ventura, already annoyed with this man's lack of terror and self-consciousness about the tavern's gossip, dragged him by the arm towards the entrance.

"Let's take this outside." Vito followed close behind them. Ventura then slammed the tavern door. "¿Qué fue eso?" she demanded. "What was that?"

The stranger, regaining his composure, replied, "Sorry, I've just always wanted to meet one of your kind. This is fascinating; you can be out in broad daylight!"

"My *kind?* ¿Qué estás tratando de decir con eso? What are you trying to say with that?!" He stared at her, surprised by her outburst. She sighed in frustration— humans truly knew nothing about monsters. "¿Quién eres tú para decirme algo?" The man stared at Ventura blankly. She rolled her eyes in annoyance. "Who are you to ask me anything?"

The man extended his arm to her. "My name is Omair, I'm investigating a case." Ventura looked down at his hand without taking it.

"What does that have to do with me being a vampire?" She asked expectantly.

Omair gave a sheepish smile as he retracted his hand. "Well....nothing really. I'm just a big fan of monsters, I guess."

While Ventura was unsure how to react to this human's odd behavior, she ultimately concluded that he wasn't much of a threat to her or society.

"How about we do this: you go back to whoever hired you and tell them Edmund was murdered by thieves, bandits, or whatever. You can keep my secret, and I promise not to kill you. Deal?" Ventura extended her hand to Omair.

Omair looked down at her hand. He smiled and took it. "Deal, but you also have to answer my vampire questions before you go."

Ventura rolled her eyes again. "Fine."

Chapter 2

Leaving Verona was harder than the last time Ventura left. She had wanted to spend more time with everyone at the tavern, telling them about her latest escapade. Vito noticed her slight frown as they strolled on the path to Devontae. He barked at her, causing Ventura to look down at him.

"What is it, perrihijo?" He barked again and ran near a tree to get a stick. Vito returned and set it down. He barked once with his tail wagging.

Ventura picked up the stick and waved it in the air, "You want the stick, Chupie?" Vito barked in response. "Okay, well, go get it!" Ventura threw the stick half a mile into the distance. Vito sped off to go retrieve it.

Ventura chuckled to herself. Vito always managed to bring a smile to her face when she was disheartened. Though even as she watched Vito leave, she couldn't help but think back to the strange man from the tavern. How had he managed to find her?

She didn't think anyone would care enough to find out what had happened to someone like Edmund. It was common knowledge amongst anyone who knew him that he was someone unpleasant. Also, what kind of human wasn't afraid of a vampire? He didn't seem to understand how dangerous it was to be in her presence.

Ventura was so caught off guard by his behavior that she left immediately after answering his questions. Yet even so, she had also found him somewhat charming. He was the first person who hadn't been afraid of her after finding out what she was. It was nice to have someone not be scared of her for once. She assumed that's what being a real human was like. People weren't always running away from you in fear. She wasn't just a monster to him.

Ventura reached for the cross around her neck. "Just like back home," she whispered to herself.

Vito's footsteps could be heard in the distance as he sprinted towards her. Ventura kneeled down on one knee so Vito could run into her embrace. She wrapped her arms around him tightly, then rubbed the little fur on his head.

"Buen chico."

****

Princess Aria stood before her court as they began to leave the room. She had her eyes on Giles as he left.

Ever since her brother had become king, the kingdom had gone into a disarranged state. The royal court had been wasting money on parties galore, overtaxing the citizens to the point of destitution, and prisoners were disappearing from the dungeons. There were also suspicious burnings nearby at night. She had tried to set things right for the kingdom financially, but none of the others seemed to understand the consequences of these decisions. In order to afford parties, the royal court was overtaxing the kingdom, but the commonwealth was in such poverty that the country was going further into debt.

The princess had hired Omair to investigate the mysterious disappearance of the prisoners and Ventura to execute Giles— a noble who had not only contributed the most to the kingdom's debt but had also imprisoned many innocent townspeople.

She only recently discovered that Giles and a few other nobles were not only taking advantage of the citizens' taxes and using them for their own personal gatherings but also imprisoning innocent commoners behind her back. When she found out, she immediately went to her brother Charles, but he merely dismissed her findings as gossip and nothing more. It didn't matter to her sisters either. No one would listen to her concerns. So she decided to take matters into her own hands.

Aimon came up beside the princess. "The inquisitor is here to see you."

"Let him in."

Aimon nodded and opened the door for Omair to enter. "Your Royal Highness." He bowed.

"Greetings, Omair." She made her way toward him as she waved Aimon away. "I'm sure you heard the news," Omair said with a sigh.

Aria nodded. "I have, but I still need you. Your job remains the same. I need you to find out who else is involved with the prisoners' disappearances."

Omair nodded in agreement. "Of course, princess." He said, a bit disappointed in himself for not finding more information.

"I will pay you double for your troubles."

"Thank you, Your Highness," Omair said sheepishly. The princess smiled at him graciously. Omair was essential to fixing the problem since she couldn't get information from her own court.

"I'm grateful that we can speak alone since the other nobles of the court are making their way to the social gathering in Euganea."

Aimon interrupted by opening the door again, "Ventura has arrived, your majesty."

The princess turned to Omair. "Thank you, but it's time you leave. I have other matters to attend to. I promise we'll meet again soon." Omair was about to speak when Aimon escorted him out of the room by the arm.

Omair had heard of the assassin Ventura but had never seen her. She was one of the great legends that people would always speak of. Stories said she could slice a man in half in less than a second. To hire her was an honor in itself.

Aimon could see the interest in his eyes. "I can have you wait in the hall if you want to meet Ventura." Omair stared at him in stunned disbelief.

"Oh, could you? I would love to meet her!" Aimon covered Omair's mouth to hush him.

"Alright, alright, but keep it down. I don't want to get in trouble for allowing it." Omair nodded through Aimon's grasp.

He left Omair standing by the door at a distance. Omair managed to catch sight of the princess speaking to someone with a familiar dark hood, but she disappeared behind the door once they reached the room.

Chapter 3

Ventura closed the door behind her and Princess Aria. The princess looked down at Vito with an enlivened expression. "I see you've brought your canine companion with you."

She grinned. "Never leave without him."

The princess turned her attention to the papers on the table. "I appreciate you coming with such short notice and little information. I had to keep it confidential." Those words were familiar to Ventura.

"I understand."

The princess reached for the stack of papers and handed them to Ventura. "As you know, I need you to execute someone. The papers you hold in your hands are for who you'll be killing. I understand that you investigate before accepting a job, but I've gone and done that for you."

Ventura looked through the papers carefully. "This is very well done," she said, impressed.

The princess looked up at Ventura. "Ventura, I need to know that I can count on you to complete this mission."

Ventura paused and stared at the princess silently before responding, "I can do it." The princess looked relieved to hear Ventura say those words. Ventura put the papers in her bag quickly. "I should leave now, I don't want to cause any suspicion."

"Don't worry, you can relax. The nobles have gone to another gathering, and my brother is overseas at the moment, meeting with the ruler of another kingdom." The princess assured her. "You can leave through the hall." Ventura opened the door and whistled for Vito to follow.

"Before you go, Ventura," she looked back at the princess, "be careful." Ventura gave her a gentle nod of assurance before leaving.

Omair, who had been waiting near the door, walked up to Ventura abruptly, causing her to draw her sword.

"Woah!" Omair lifted both his arms in a plea motion. Once Ventura realized who it was, she withdrew her sword quickly. "It's you!" Omair said, astonished.

"Yes, it's me again. But I have no time to waste, I have a job to do. So con permiso." Ventura tried to move past Omair, but he moved right in front of her.

"But you're Ventura, the master of swords!" Ventura tried to move past him once more, but he moved with her. "The killer of feinds!" Ventura moved back. but Omair stepped forward. "The battle angel of the night!"

Ventura placed her hand over his mouth. "Alright. Yes, that's me, now keep it down," she whispered.

She released her grasp, then made her way to the door. Ventura expected Omair to leave now that he'd seen her, but he continued to follow her.

"Why did the princess need to speak with the great Ventura? Is there trouble? Did she hire you?"

Ventura was tempted to shush him again, but Vito intervened and ran in front of Omair playfully. Before she could tell him to stop, Omair was petting and playing with him. It caused Ventura to break into a laugh. "You're not like most other people, are you?"

Omair shook his head joyfully. "Not really, but neither are you." Ventura couldn't argue with that. She was nothing like anyone else.

"I just mean most people don't like the Xoloitzcuintli breed."

Omair chuckled. "I find this breed fascinating. Did you know its name originated from the Aztecs?" Ventura nodded. Omair then stood up. "Why did the princess *really* speak to you?"

Ventura didn't really want to tell him anything. She knew nothing about this man. She had only met him today. He may have seemed nice, but she knew people could be deceitful.

Omair stared at her eyes, which were covered by a shadow of doubt. He wanted to prove his trustworthiness to her. He knew Ventura was known for her goodwill from the people, so he didn't fear her.

"I'm Inquisitor Omair from Venetia. I was hired by the princess to investigate the missing prisoners of the kingdom. That's why I needed to know who wanted to kill Edmund."

Omair pulled out the papers he had received from the princess and handed them to her. from the princess when he was first instructed to watch over Edmund. Ventura grabbed them and recognized the princess's handwriting. Even if Omair was telling the truth, why was he so interested in her? He obviously had his own mission.

She handed him back the papers. "I understand, but I have my own instructions from the princess that I have to complete. Have a good day." Ventura whistled for Vito to move with her.

As she started to leave, Omair chased after her shadow. "Who does she want you to execute?"

Ventura didn't stop walking this time. "It's confidential, Omair." Her pace got quicker, and so did Vito's, but Omair didn't stop following. He knew whoever the princess wanted gone could be a crucial piece to the puzzle.

He continued pleading with Ventura until she caught sight of Giles's carriage. She caught his scent but couldn't speed after it in broad daylight with all the guards present. She quickly looked around for a horse she could use but saw none. Omair noticed her desperation and placed a hand on her shoulder. "Is everything alright?" Ventura turned to Omair. "Do you know where Giles is headed?"

Omair stared at the carriage for a moment. "If I recall correctly, he's headed to one of the royal court's social gatherings in Euganea." Ventura groaned. "If that's who you're after, I could use your assistance."

She wasn't really in the mood to hear his request, but seeing as her target was getting away, she didn't think she had much of a choice. "What do you want?"

"I need a favor." Ventura looked at Omair, clearly unamused. Omair began to explain. "I think Giles is more use to my case alive rather than dead. We can find him and solve the mystery together."

Ventura looked back at the papers the princess had given her. She could see how Giles could be related to the problem and have information, but her job was to get rid of him. Ventura couldn't see the princess being happy about keeping Giles alive.

"I know she wants him gone, but if you could just let me get what I need from him, that would be great." Ventura didn't see the harm in that, but having him tag along would only slow her down even more. She would have to take more time to keep Omair alive— he would just be another burden to carry.

Vito knew she would refuse, and he pushed her towards Omair with his head. Ventura looked at him. He pointed his snout towards Omair as if to say *Bring him.* Seeing as her canine wanted him to join, she agreed, but with a condition. "I get half the money the princess gives you, and I get to kill whoever else is behind the missing prisoners."

Omair agreed so they shook on it. "I can't wait to get started."

Chapter 4

Since Omair knew the location of Euganea, Ventura allowed him to lead. They would make their journey on foot. It would take Ventura an additional three days to arrive, while she could have arrived by nightfall on her own. She stayed patient with Omair since she was getting paid and receiving a free meal from it.

They decided to leave the next morning at seven. Ventura bought a room at the Crimson Inn for the night, where she stayed with Vito after they went to hunt for their dinner.

Omair stayed in a room not far from hers. There he lay in bed, excited for whatever tomorrow would bring. He never lit a candle; he managed to find his way in the dark perfectly fine. The dark was comforting to him, the shadows like a language he had known all his life.

Ventura lit a candle just for the familiar sense of home. She missed it but knew that she was where she needed to be. Snuggled next to her was Vito, fast asleep. Ventura opened her small notebook to add the last phrase of a melody she had been working on. She smiled to herself in the darkness. "Perfecto," she said as she finished writing the last line.

She then placed the notebook back in her bag and lay down next to Vito, staring at the fire before she slowly drifted off into a deep slumber.

****

Ventura awoke to the sound of crying. She sat upright in her bed and looked around her room. She found Vito laying next to her with his ears up and alert. He had heard it, too, so she knew she hadn't imagined it. They both got up from the bed and went towards the door.

Outside, there was nothing but a night's chilling cold breeze. It was still dark in the sky, but Ventura sensed that there was something else. She stepped outside and looked around until she caught sight of a little girl huddled into a little ball in the corner nearby.

Ventura walked over to her and sat down beside her. "What's the matter, mija?" The girl looked up to reveal a stream of red tears on her face. Ventura grabbed her face in her hands in a panic. "Who did this to you?"

She sniffed. "I'm fine. My mom got it worse." Ventura didn't understand. "The guards took her earlier. I tried to stop them, but I got cut on my face.... I couldn't stop them." The little girl burst into tears once more.

Ventura held her tightly. "It's okay, I'm here." Omair had come outside to see what all the commotion was and saw Ventura holding the child. She looked at the little girl in the eyes. "Where did the guards go?"

The little girl sniffed again. "They were headed for the alley."

Ventura got a sick feeling in her stomach. "Where?"

With her small hand, she pointed north. Ventura nodded. "Omair, Vito, stay with the girl. I'm going after her."

Omair tried to protest by saying, "Ventura, let's think about this—" but Ventura was already disappearing into the mist.

****

Guards surrounded the young woman. "Please, I have a child!" she begged. They laughed and hit her once more, pushing her up against the wall as she tried to fight back, knowing that she was no match for these men. She prepared for the pain she would endure, but Ventura appeared from the fog.

One guard saw her and, with a drunken voice, scoffed, "Lookit, someone's gotta problem wit us."

Ventura looked up from her hood. "Actually, I do." She moved her cloak to draw her sword. The other guards were now looking at her.

"She's just a girl. What is she gonna do?" One pointed his fat finger at her, and they started to laugh. Ventura smiled.

She stayed silent and smirked in response to the guard's ignorance.

"You think this is funny?" Ventura looked up at him.

"Un poco." She grinned. Upon hearing that, one guard got angry and drew his sword. He lunged at her, but he couldn't compete with Ventura's speed. When he missed, she tripped him with her leg. He hit the floor with a splat. Ventura then kicked off his armor to slice through his skin. As she cut across his stomach, organs and bits of intestines started to spill upon the cold hard floor.

Ventura looked back at the other guards. Now they were angry too, and they all came at her. Ventura dodged their swings and glided over them to block the young maiden from their grasp.

She held her sword firmly and sliced the men from their sides. One of them grabbed her cloak and tried pulling her to the ground, but she turned and sliced his hand completely off. He screamed in agony as he fell to the floor.

When she was sure that all ten guards were down, she turned to the mother, who was shaking. "Are you okay?" Ventura asked calmly.

The woman looked up at her. She stepped back nervously, causing her to trip. Ventura pulled down her hood so the woman could see her face. She could see Ventura's short dark hair and eyes of compassion. Ventura put her sword down so the woman could see that she meant no harm.

Ventura raised both empty hands in front of her. "See? I'm not going to harm you." The woman began to sob vigorously. Ventura knelt down and hugged her. "You're safe now."

"I-I was so scared....I thought they were going to....." The woman's voice trailed off as she pictured what could have happened.

Ventura gave a gentle nod and sat beside the women. "It's okay, you don't have to say it."

The mother wiped her tears away from her eyes. "I'm just glad they took me and not my daughter." Once the mother realized, she grabbed Vetura frantically. "Where is my daughter?"

Ventura gently grabbed the woman's hands in her to calm her. "Don't worry, she's waiting by the Inn. I'll take you to her." Ventura helped the woman to her feet and led her to the Crimson Inn, where Omair and the girl were waiting. When the girl caught sight of her mother, she ran to her, and they embraced each other desperately.

"I thought I'd lost you!" the girl cried. The mother shook her head through tears in her eyes.

"You could never lose me, Lucy. I'll always be here with you." Though Ventura took part in the convivial atmosphere, it pained her to be reminded of her own mother. The woman then looked back at Ventura. "Thank you," she said graciously.

Ventura smiled. "Of course. Do you have a place to go home to?" Ventura asked. The little girl shook her head.

The mother answered, "They imprisoned my husband and took our land from us. We have no home."

Ventura thought for a moment as Vito licked the little girl's face. "Why don't you two stay with us for tonight? We'll find you a place in the morning." The mother accepted. The following morning, Ventura asked the owner of the inn if he could hire the woman to work for him and offer her housing until she could afford her own. He looked at her and was about to refuse, but Ventura displayed to him a pile of coins. "Maybe this will change your mind."

He immediately took the deal and accepted Ventura's offer. She gave the woman and her daughter one last hug before she left with Omair and Vito to Euganea.

As Ventura gave one last wave to the people, Omair watched in awe. He walked close behind her. "How do you do it?"

Ventura didn't understand his question. "What do you mean?"

Omair wasn't sure how to answer her. "Well....you helped that family so naturally."

She smiled. "I fight for the good of the people." Ventura continued walking calmly while Omair just watched her with a quiet admiration.

He knew working with her had been the right decision.

Chapter 5

Vito was happy to finally have new company in the group. He often barked at Omair, trying to get his attention in any kind of way to play or just be acknowledged. Omair had packed nothing other than a few clothes, some coins, and a grin that would brighten anyone's day.

He walked up beside Ventura. "So, where did a vampire like you learn to sword fight?"

Ventura thought for a moment. "When I was younger and first starting out as an assassin, I traveled to many different countries where I studied the art of swordsmanship."

"Oh, how enchanting! What styles do you know?"

"I know Baritisu, Kenjutsu, Iaijutsu, and a few others." Ventura thought back to when she was first practicing with swords at fifteen. She had been struggling with her swings for hours in the forest near Venetia when Grant had come to check on her.

"You okay, kid?"

Ventura shook her head. "I can't do it, Grant."

Grant walked over to Ventura with his arms crossed. "You can't do what, exactly?"

Ventura sighed. "I'm not swinging it right. It's supposed to go like this." She lifted the sword and swung it at a tree. "But it's all messed up!"

Grant chuckled and grabbed the sword. "You mean like this?" Grant swung the sword and sliced the trunk of the tree completely in half.

Ventura nodded. "¡Sí, exactamente así!"

Grant smiled and grabbed Ventura's hands in his. He guided her arms to move the sword properly. "You have to move it like this. See?"

Ventura nodded. "Ah, okay." She then proceeded to draw the sword, then jump towards a tree, and cut the trunk clean off.

The tree fell with a loud thud. Grant applauded. "Well done, Ventura."

She smiled at him. "Couldn't have done it without you, Grant."

"So why use swords and not your vampire strengths?" asked Omair.

Ventura smiled. "I try to blend in."

Omair wanted to ask more but refrained from overwhelming her with his questions. He felt like he'd done enough of that already. He was aware that sometimes he didn't know when to quit talking.

Though Ventura didn't mind his talking at all. Not many people were interested in getting to know more about her. Certain things she didn't mind sharing, others not so much. Omair could understand trying to fit in. He had always been a bit of an outcast himself. He was better at problem-solving than people. The only reason he had become an inquisitor was because cases were just mysteries to be solved. While Ventura was invested more in people, Omair focused on puzzles.

Ventura looked at the position of the sun. It looked to be around eight in the morning. Omair had led the group through the woods as a shortcut, but he hadn't planned for breakfast. "I think it's time we stop to eat."

Omair stopped walking. "Now? But there are no shops for food nearby." Ventura searched the trees and caught sight of some fruits and maple. Then she looked to the bushes for berries.

She told Vito to find a river stream for water and pulled out her sword. Omair wasn't sure what Ventura's plan was until she ran up the tree to cut the fruits clean off the branches. Her feet landed gently on the soil so she could catch the falling fruits. Omair was captivated by Ventura's swiftness.

Then she grabbed a leaf from a branch and threw the fruits in the air once more to slice them into various smaller pieces. Using the leaf she'd found, she caught the remainder of the fruit.

Ventura added some berries over it before grabbing a stick to get some maple from the tree. She drizzled some over the fruit. Once she finished, she wrapped the ingredients within the leaf and handed it to Omair.

He stood there, silently confused. "It's a tasty fruit roll. You eat it." Omair gently took the wrap as Vito returned.

Vito barked to get Ventura's attention. "Did you find the river?" He nodded and barked again.

The three of them made their way to the river, where they decided to eat. Upon taking a bite, Omair's mouth was flushed with a wave of flavor. "This is delicious!"

Ventura gave a knowing nod. "Told you."

"Thank you."

She only smiled and ate her wrap. Vito decided to eat the fruit separately without the leaf.

"Where did you learn to make this?"

Ventura chewed quietly before answering. "I made it up."

"How do you know which fruits aren't poisonous?"

Ventura smiled. "I don't."

Omair stopped mid-bite of his wrap. He looked down in horror at what he had just bitten into. He could feel his face getting hot and his heart pounding.

He turned back to Ventura, who burst into laughter. "Cálmate rubio, I'm just kidding. Of course, I know they aren't poisonous." Omair gave a nervous smile while Ventura was laughing on her side. "You should've seen your face, though! You were petrified!"

Omair stopped pretending to be amused and glared at her. "I was worried that you unknowingly poisoned us."

Ventura shook her head. "I've been living off the land long enough to know how to survive it." Omair thought about her words for a moment.

"How long?"

Ventura didn't respond immediately. She remembered the town of San Joaquin, but after that, she had been on her own. She had always technically lived off the land. She survived on fruits, vegetables, and the livestock of farmers throughout her life. Ventura couldn't think of a time when she didn't hunt or make her food herself. Ever since she had been with her mother, she could recognize different plants and herbs to make potions, soups, and natural remedies.

Omair was still waiting for her answer. "Forever, I guess," was all she managed to say. She looked at the sun again. "Looks like it's almost nine. We should start moving." They gathered their things to start walking again.

Ventura walked slightly ahead of Omair to avoid any more questions of her past. Instead, she asked him to share a bit more about himself. Since he was so interested in getting personal, she decided to let him do the talking for the both of them.

Omair openly shared some of his past. He had grown up an only child to a single father, who had told him that his mother had passed away when he was born, but he had later discovered the truth. His father was stern and cold. He raised Omair to live away from people rather than with them.

They had lived in the outskirts of Venetia. While his father was away at work, Omair would sneak out to go visit the townspeople. Even then, they had outcasted him for being different from them. Omair enjoyed figuring out puzzles and questioning everything. Thus, he was shunned to the point where he returned home, hoping to one day be accepted.

It wasn't until he was old enough to leave and make his own life that he left Venetia to pursue a job as an inquisitor. Even though he was welcomed into society, it bothered him that they only accepted him as a servant of the people and nothing more. He had come to realize that he was replaceable.

Ventura stopped walking abruptly, which surprised Omair. She looked at Omair long and hard for a few seconds before speaking. "How could you ever think that you're replaceable?"

Omair shrugged. "Well, I just put the puzzle pieces together in a case. Anyone can do that."

"¿En serio? Are you for real?" Omair was confused. Duna shook her head in disbelief. "You found Ventura, *the* Ventura, just based off of a few sword markings. Not just anyone can do that." She said as she motioned to Omair.

Omair looked away sheepishly. "I suppose."

Ventura gently grabbed his shoulder. "Know your worth." Omair stared at her hand, feeling flustered before she released him and kept walking. "Now come on, we don't have all day."

Omair obediently followed, wearing a smile on his face.

Chapter 6

The sky began to dim, and Ventura decided that they would make camp for the night. She told Omair to start gathering branches to start a fire.

Ventura started collecting large branches from trees to try to build a bed above the ground. She hummed along to herself as she'd done on previous travels. She then tied the branches together using a string of cloth she had for sewing. When that was finished, Vito grabbed her some leaves to use as a mattress to cover the sticks she would sleep on.

She then used the blanket she brought as a roof over the bed in case of rain. Once the main part of the bed was ready, Vito helped her grab parts off bushes and leaves to surround her little bed area so it would blend in with the forest. Vito would sleep under her on the ground, where he would also be sheltered. She took a step back to admire her work.

Once Omair returned with the branches, both beds were set up. "You know how to build shelter, too?"

Ventura nodded. "I lived in the forest for a good while."

Omair touched the leaves on the outside of the fort. "It's incredible."

Vito barked in agreement. Ventura saw the moon rising overhead in the distance and tensed. Wolves would be out, so if Vito and she were to hunt, they had to do it now. "Omair, you start the fire. Vito and I are gonna get food." Ventura then whistled for Vito.

Omair hesitated. "I....uh..." Ventura faced back toward him.

"You do know how, right?" Omair shook his head gently. Ventura sighed. She got down next to Omair and showed him.

Using two sticks, she rubbed them together until a spark appeared, then she threw the sticks in the pile and blew on the flame.

Once it started, Ventura whistled to Vito so they could hunt. However, Omair wanted to join them. Ventura paused.

"Maybe I could help."

Both she and Vito exchanged looks. "You sure you won't freak out?" Omair nodded enthusiastically. Ventura looked at Vito, who barked his approval. "Alright, well, Vito says you can join, but if you faint, that's on you."

Omair laughed, not entirely sure if she was kidding this time. Ventura led them both into the woods and sniffed the air. She then gracefully flew up a tree while Vito hid in the bushes.

This left Omair exposed. Not sure what to do, he stood behind a tree, but he still peeked his head out so he could observe the hunt.

Everything was silent for a few minutes until Omair heard the sound of a branch breaking from a nearby bush. Out came a deer that stepped in the middle of the moonlight. It lowered its head to eat the grass below it.

Omair smiled until Ventura whistled, and Vito sprinted towards the deer. As he did, he transformed into a larger version of himself: sprouting out large spikes from his back and bearing fangs as sharp as knives.

Before it had the chance to run, Vito pounced on it within seconds. He dug his fangs into its neck and slurped its blood like an ice cream on a hot summer's day. From the moment Vito bit into the deer, its body went limp, and Omair could physically see the body stiffen from the lack of blood.

When Vito finished, he dropped the body on the floor. Ventura then came down from the tree and looked over the deer. She kneeled over it for a few moments with her head bowed and proceeded to lift the deer's body over her shoulder as Vito followed close behind.

Ventura walked towards Omair. "Time to eat." She moved past him as he anxiously watched them in terror.

Arriving back at camp, Ventura returned to the river to wash the body, leaving Omair alone with Vito. Omair just stared at him silently. By now, Vito had transformed back into his normal dog form. He was panting with his tongue hanging out.

"I *just* pet you," Omair said with a tone of disbelief.

Vito stopped panting and tilted his head in confusion. The canine had honestly expected Omair to have figured out that he wasn't an ordinary animal by now since he was traveling with Ventura.

Omair was quiet until Ventura returned with the washed animal. "Time to start cooking!" She began to skin the animal while singing to herself quietly as Omair tried to form the words he wanted to say.

"Um....Ventura?"

Without looking up from her work, she responded with, "Mm?"

"When you said that...um...Vito wasn't a dog.... What did you say he was again..?" Ventura looked up and smiled at Vito, who barked so she could tell Omair. "He's a chupacabra."

Omair's heart dropped. He looked back at Vito, who was panting again, but he relaxed when he remembered who he had come with. It made sense. He needed blood like her, which is why he wasn't afraid. "That...actually makes sense."

Ventura chuckled and started to cut the meat into smaller pieces. "I found Vito near Verona. He was feeding off some livestock when I saw him." She thought back to that late December night.

She was thirteen at the time and had recently started to go by the name Ventura. *The only reason she had been in Verona was to visit Grant, but she was about to leave when she heard slurping. She looked around in the darkness, only having the moonlight to guide her footsteps.*

Ventura, being the curious girl she was, followed the sound. When she turned the corner, she saw a small creature over a sheep. Once the creature finished draining the sheep, it dropped the animal with a thud. Ventura cautiously walked closer to catch a better glimpse.

The beast made eye contact. He froze, expecting Ventura to charge at him or scream like so many others have. So he was surprised when she remained calm. She slowly made her way towards him.

Standing there below the moon, she could finally see him clearly. He was a black dog with spike-like fur around his back and neck. His eyes were a bright baby blue. She sat down beside him and took off her hood.

He took a step back. "Oye, está bien." She lifted her lip to reveal her own fangs. "I'm just like you."

The creature relaxed beside her. Ventura touched the sheep's motionless body. She gently touched where he had bitten the creature. He'd left bite marks. "You drank her blood, didn't you?" He hung his head in shame, expecting her to scold him. Instead, she petted him. He looked up in confusion. He didn't expect to be rewarded for his behavior.

She giggled. "I do that too, but to people." Ventura pointed to a man in an alley nearby. The dog gave a small nod of understanding. "Me gustas. I like you." The dog licked her face to say he felt the same, and in that moment, Ventura made a decision that would make her world all the more joyful. "I'm keeping you." He snuggled up beside her. "And your name will be Vito," she said kindly.

Omair, after overcoming his terror, said, "Hey can I help with the deer meat?" Ventura snapped back into the present and turned to Omair.

"Está bien. Alright."

Chapter 7

Omair helped cook the meat well and threw the bones near Vito so he could chew them. Ventura served the food for both her and Omair and bowed her head to pray before eating. Omair felt bad eating before her, so he waited for her to finish.

He didn't know that vampires could be religious in any way, given the rumors. When Ventura ended her prayer, she caught Omair watching her. "I grew up Catholic." She said nothing more about it after that.

Once they had finished their dinner, Ventura took off her cloak. Omair looked up, a bit stunned.

He noticed how her hair was darker than shadows but how her eyes sparkled like the stars themselves. Though he had seen her skin vaguely under her cloak, he could clearly see how she was the color of cinnamon, not caramel.

Her hair ended right by her ears and had a poofy look. Her nose was small, and her eyes looked like ocean pearls. Her figure was curvy and petite. He smiled as he noticed how tiny she really was.

She was breathtaking, but it had been hard to tell from under her cloak. He assumed she wore it to give off a more ominous appearance. It did make her more threatening, he just thought it was a shame that she hid her beauty.

Ventura noticed him staring at her. "Yes?"

Omair gushed instantly. "Nothing!" he sputtered.

Ventura looked at him awkwardly. "Um, okay." She slowly started to take off her armor, which made Omair turn away, embarrassed.

"Um, do you want some privacy to change?"

Ventura turned to Omair casually and said, "I just need to do something real quick." She rolled up her shoulder sleeve to remove a patch with red markings.

Omair turned to look at it. "What's that?"

Ventura stared at Omair. "It's a blood patch, I have to renew it. I haven't had blood today, so I need it to keep me stable."

Omair sat silently, observing her. She removed the old patch and added a new one. She then rolled down her sleeve to cover her shoulder once more.

"Where do you get them from?" She wasn't sure how to tell Omair the truth without him getting concerned. Omair assured her it was fine.

"They have them in the black market. They're expensive, though, so I only have so many." Omair didn't ask anything more about the patch.

As an assassin, she was able to afford to purchase the patches. Not long after becoming Ventura did she realize that she couldn't solely survive off the humans as prey. She often grew hungry from the few jobs she received and needed to have blood at least once a day to avoid a blood withdrawal. It was becoming harder for her until one day she heard rumors of patches. Ventura was desperate to get them. She only used them for emergencies like now since animals were scarce in this part of the woods.

Ventura set her armor aside before she sat down beside the fire. Omair moved closer to her and looked to the sky. Vito sat a few feet away.

"You see anything?"

Omair looked at Ventura. "Like constellations?"

Ventura laughed. "No, I mean pictures in the sky. Constellations are nice, but it's nice to make up your own."

Omair gave it a try. He stared up at the sky and pointed toward the north star. "If you connect the north star with the ones next to it, they look like a dragon."

Ventura tilted her head and squinted at it for a while. "I think I see it." She pointed to the opposite end of the sky. "You see that one? It looks like a troll."

Omair could see it clearly. "It does!" They both laughed.

They spent a few more minutes pointing out other things they saw until Ventura said, "Reminds me of when I used to look at the sky with my mamá." Omair looked at Ventura. He hadn't thought about if she ever had a mother or a family. He couldn't imagine how she had ended up being alone.

"You visit her?"

Ventura tensed. She turned away from Omair slightly. "She's gone."

Omair tried to ask further. "What happened?"

Vito saw the tears forming in Ventura's eyes. She thought back to the fire and the screams from San Joaquin. She remembered running, fearing for her life. Her lungs were starting to close in, she had a slight shortness of breath. She immediately stood up to dust herself off to regain her composure.

"We should get some rest. We have a long way to go." Ventura motioned for Vito to come to bed.

"But we were -"

"Night, Omair," Ventura interrupted, obviously cutting the conversation short.

Omair watched her leave sadly. "Night, Ventura."

Chapter 8

Ventura lay motionless on her bed of branches. She turned over to see Omair sleeping in his space. She had tried falling asleep while reading over her poems in the songbook, but she found sleep nearly impossible.

So she pushed the leaf roof aside to stare at the stars. She couldn't sleep, not after thinking about her mother.

Vito heard Ventura turning in her bed and looked up at her. Ventura sighed. She wiped the tears from her eyes and sat up as she put her notebook away again. "I'm going for a hunt." She took her blood patch off and folded it to save it for another emergency.

Vito stood up, prepared to follow her, but Ventura refused. "No, tienes que quedarte aquí para proteger a este." She pointed to Omair, who was sleeping so soundly he had begun to snore. Her chupacabra sat down obediently. Though he wasn't very happy about her going into the woods alone, he didn't argue.

Ventura grabbed her swords and cloak to speed off into the night. She searched to find anything alive but found nothing. She kept running in hopes that she wouldn't think

about the flames anymore, but the memories kept flooding back. All she could see was the moonlight that fell over her.

She finally sat down to take a breath. Ventura pulled her knees to her chest and cradled up into a little ball like she had done the night of the fire. She grabbed her cross necklace and turned to the sky. "Por favor, Dios, déjame olvidar. Al menos por esta noche."

As if answering a prayer, a bird fell into Ventura's lap. The bird had a cut across its chest and was dying. Ventura grabbed it in her hands to slowly calm the bird. "I can help." The bird caught sight of her teeth and backed away but stopped panicking when it realized it was going to die either way. It lay there with its eyes closed, facing away from her as a way of granting permission. Ventura gently bit into the bird and drained the remainder of its blood so it could die quickly. She quietly thanked it for its sacrifice. With her free hand, Ventura made a small hole and placed the bird in it. She bowed her head in respect and prayed that it made it to heaven safely. With that small prayer, she covered the bird so it could be one with the land again.

She smiled under the twilight sky but sensed something in the shadows watching her. Ventura grabbed her sword and got on her feet. "Who goes there?" she demanded, but was only met with silence.

She relaxed when she saw a small bunny jump out from the bushes. The bunny looked up at her, then, with a twitch of its nose, disappeared again. Ventura couldn't help but laugh at herself for being so naive.

Nothing else was in these woods but her. Yet as much as she wanted to believe that, she knew it wasn't true.

She withdrew her weapon and made her way back to the campsite, where she saw Omair still fast asleep.

Vito was still awake, waiting for her. Ventura set her things down and lay back down. "We should rest for real now." Vito licked Ventura's nose. She smiled. "Buenas noches, perrihijo."

****

Omair was awakened by the sunlight peeking through the shade of leaves over his bed. He sat up only to see Ventura cooking some fish over the fire. "Good morning."

"Morning." He rubbed his eyes, trying to shake the exhaustion off. He noticed how her mood had changed completely from last night. She already had her armor on, and it seemed like she'd been awake for a while. Ventura wore everything but her cloak, so he had the chance to appreciate her beauty a bit longer.

"Where did you get fish from?"

"From the river." She flipped the fish on its other side. "Want some?" Omair nodded.

For the past two days, Ventura had been responsible for forging food. So Omair promised himself that he would handle the meals once they reached the nearest village. The last thing he wanted was for Ventura to think that he couldn't carry his own weight.

He sat down to eat beside her. "We're almost near the end of the forest. There's a town nearby. We can stay there for the night."

Ventura nodded. "Sounds like a plan."

They ate silently until Omair spoke again. "I saw that you disappeared last night. I got worried for a bit."

Ventura didn't meet his eyes. "I needed a walk." Omair tried to think of something else to say, but he didn't want to push her away again like he had last night. Vito barked when he finished his food, and Ventura cleaned the mess. Omair made sure to help take everything down to cover their tracks.

Today, Omair took the lead while Ventura walked further behind. She couldn't shake off the creature that she had sensed in the woods. She felt like she had been followed back to camp, but she found it odd that Omair had realized she'd left. She was certain that he had been asleep.

Ventura looked up at Omair, who smiled back at her. He was sweet, but she had to keep her distance. She tried to distract her mind by focusing on the path ahead, but Omair continued to stare at her. It made her slightly uncomfortable, so she pulled her hood over her face. Vito noticed and pulled her cloak with his teeth.

Ventura pulled her cloak away from him in annoyance, but Vito pulled once more. *¿Qué haces ahora?* she thought as she glared at him.

Vito pointed to her face. *Quit being so defensive,* he seemed to say. Ventura groaned and reluctantly removed her cloak to reveal her twilight-colored hair. *¿Estás feliz ahora?* she thought as she motioned to her head. Vito gave his nod of approval. For an animal, he sure had a lot of opinions.

Though Omair never took his eyes off of her, he kept quiet about it, which made the trip more bearable for Ventura.

They reached the town in the late evening. When they arrived, Ventura took a look around. She'd never been here before, so this was new to her.

"Welcome to Jacaranda." Omair said as Ventura gave a slight grin.

Omair led her to the shops on the street corner, where they were selling food and supplies. Ventura caught sight of a modrý fruit called from a nearby cart and went to pull out her coins, but Omair intervened. "I got this." He handed the man a portion of his coins and gave the fruit to Ventura.

She accepted the fruit and tried to pay Omair back, but he lifted his hand in refusal. "No." Ventura was about to protest, but he stopped her. "Please, I insist. Consider it a thank you for everything you did in the forest."

She wasn't sure how to respond, so she just gave a quiet *Thank you* and continued walking through the street, but she had her wallet at the ready to pay. Ventura didn't rely on

others, much less for purchases. She was usually the one helping others, never the one being helped.

Anytime Ventura found something she was interested in buying, Omair stepped in to pay for it almost immediately. She was always startled when he jumped in front of her to handle it. Eventually, she just stepped back to let him. He was more than happy to take this opportunity to prove that he was capable of taking a load off her shoulders.

Ventura smiled anytime he bought her something to show that she was grateful, but she felt bad for accepting his help.

Omair could tell that it made Ventura uneasy to be cared for, so he allowed her to choose where they would stay for the night.

Yet before she paid, he gently grabbed her hand to stop her. Ventura tensed and turned to Omair. "I got you, don't worry."

She relaxed when he released her and walked her to the room. Omair said his goodbyes for the night; as he started to leave, Ventura called out to him. "Omair?"

He paused for a moment to acknowledge her. "Yes?"

Ventura's throat went dry, and her clothes felt tight.

"Um, I-I appreciate what you did for me today. Thank you for helping me get what I needed." Omair smiled kindly.

"Of course." He was about to leave again, but he turned to her once more. "I'm always here for you if you need it, ok?"

Ventura's eyes watered a bit. "Thanks," she said as she slowly closed her room door.

Chapter 9

Omair sat alone in his room in the darkness. He sat reminiscing about his past, thinking about his father and about the mother he never had. He had grown up alone, but that never really changed. Even now, as an inquisitor, he was solitary; his title was recognizable, yet he had no personal ties or relations to anyone else.

When he left Venetia all those years ago, he had left resenting his father. He had cursed him for raising him in isolation. If Omair dared to talk back to his father, he was met with a slap across his face. He was angry at him for keeping him away from the world when he knew more than anyone how he desperately wanted to see it. He was angry for the lashes every time Omair left without permission or disobeyed him.

He could still feel the marks on his back as he reached to touch them in the darkness. He could still hear his father's yells telling him how much he deserved it, how much he cared for him.

He was angry that his father had lied about his mother. He had discovered that his mother had abandoned him the day he was born. She realized that she couldn't live with a man like his father, but she couldn't take Omair with her since he was just a reminder of the life she was trying to leave behind.

He hated his father for not telling him the truth, instead finding out through the rumors of the village.

Omair's father had lived his whole life with a broken heart, thus causing him to raise his son in solitude. He would always tell Omair that being alone was better than being around bad company. While there was truth to what his father said, he was wrong to take it to such an extreme.

Now Omair lived his life desperate for someone, anyone, to accept him. Now he was stuck with a girl who reminded him too much of his father and was oddly like his mother too.

Ventura ran away anytime anyone got close, but unlike his mother and father, she was afraid. He wasn't sure why she was afraid or of what, but she feared closeness for a reason.

He knew for a fact that Ventura didn't fear for her safety. She could easily slay him. There was something deeper than that.

Omair chuckled at the thought of her. There was just something so fascinating about her that he couldn't explain. She was everything he wanted to be and more. She was everything that his father said he couldn't be.

Ventura was sweet as honey yet cold as ice. True, at times, she was so distant it hurt her, but he was sure she had a right to be.

He thought back to her face when she had thanked him before he left her room. She had been fidgeting with her armor and couldn't maintain eye contact for very long. It was sad to think that she had been alone for so long, but he could relate to her longing for others. The difference was that he didn't shut others out. But at the first sign of closeness, she fled.

He lay down on his pillow. "Perhaps one day, she'll accept my friendship, but for now, being her acquaintance is enough." He then closed his eyes, hoping to dream of her.

****

Ventura gathered her things in the early morning. If she had been counting the days correctly, they would arrive at Eugena by nightfall.

She was ready to leave, but Omair warned her that there was nothing between Jacaranda and Eugena for miles. There was only empty terrain as far as the eye could see, with few animals on the way.

Ventura considered this and decided to purchase two sheep for her and Vito to drain on the road. Omair ran to pay, but she denied him the opportunity to do so. "You've spent enough as it is," she stated defiantly.

Omair glared. "I don't want you using your coins when I can cover it. You don't have a lot of coins as it is. You need to save for more important things."

Ventura crossed her arms. "¿Perdona? Excuse me?"

Omair felt his face flush. "I didn't mean that you couldn't afford it, I just mean-" Ventura raised her hand to stop him.

"I can handle my own finances just fine, thank you very much." She grabbed the rest of her coins and began walking away as she ordered Vito to keep a close eye on the sheep. Vito looked back at Omair with a face of pity. Omair apologized to the sheep owner, then ran over to Ventura.

He tried to speak to her, but she was moving at such a fast pace that he had trouble keeping up. Then he got an idea. "Why don't we buy a horse too? It's a long walk, and we can take less breaks."

Ventura scowled at Omair. "Horses will only slow us down. They need to be fed and have access to water. They're just another mouth to feed, and they'll leave tracks. We need to avoid being followed."

"Don't you also leave tracks? I mean, that *is* how I found you." Ventura glared at Omair.

"I may leave tracks, but I move fast enough to avoid being followed."

"But a horse can carry us when we're exhausted during the day."

"Yes, but a horse can't hide if we're in danger, nor can it help protect us. So it's pointless buying one."

Omair looked down, ashamed of his suggestion. "I understand..." Ventura was going to continue walking when Vito frowned at her.

"¿Qué?" she whispered.

Vito motioned towards Omair with his nose. *Sé amable con él, he's only trying to help you.*

Ventura sighed and made her way toward the horses. "How much?" Omair's face brightened when he heard her say that.

She returned holding a horse by its reins and handed it to Omair.

"For you." Omair stared at her, confused. "You wanted a horse, didn't you?"

Omair smiled nervously. "Well, yes, but I meant we could both ride the horse together." Ventura scoffed.

"I can walk two times faster than a horse. I have Vito to keep up with me. Now let's go."

Chapter 10

Omair tried to make light conversation with Ventura on the path, but she only responded with short and dry remarks. Vito didn't acknowledge him much, either. He stood loyally by his owner.

Omair understood how Ventura could have taken offense to his comment, but he didn't mean it rudely. Though... he *did* have more money as a highly respected inquisitor. Besides, Ventura had to save to purchase her blood patches. He didn't see why she took

offense. Omair thought that he had only stated the facts. He was trying to be a gentleman, and here she was being ungrateful for it!

Yet even wrapped up in his own anger, Omair knew that he had been wrong to insinuate that Ventura was poor. If anything, he actually admired the fact that she could survive off the land and didn't need anyone. Ventura was resilient and could handle herself. He knew that he shouldn't have been rude. In his anger, he hadn't stopped to consider how he had made her feel by trying to protect her so much. He had only thought about himself and what *he* wanted, but he never stopped to ask what she wanted.

Omair rode the horse to catch up with Ventura slowly. Ventura didn't turn to him at all. She kept her gaze forward. "The path is pretty long, huh?"

Ventura only grunted.

Omair realized that he was getting nowhere with small talk. "I'm sorry."

Ventura didn't look at him. "For what?" she said coldly.

Omair sighed. "I'm sorry for saying what I did."

"What part?"

"I'm sorry for saying that you didn't have a lot of coins. It wasn't my place to say anything. I should have respected your space and not tried to overstep."

Ventura smiled. "Yeah, that was pretty deplorable of you."

Omair nodded in agreement. "It was."

Ventura met his eyes. "I forgive you, but don't even think of doing it again," she said while pointing her sword at him directly.

He nodded nervously. Omair continued to follow her on his horse. A few moments of silence went by. "I just want you to know…." Ventura turned to Omair, prepared to jab him with her sword if he said anything more to annoy her. "I only said that because you mentioned how you save for your blood patches. I know how much you need them, so I wanted to help you cover the costs." Ventura's expression softened. "I'm very bad at making friends since I can be overbearing. I wanted to contribute to the team since you got us food and made us shelter in the forest." Omair sighed. "I'm sorry for that."

Ventura grabbed the reins of the horse and pulled it close to her, which startled Omair. She leaned her head closer to him. "Don't beat yourself up about it. Besides, I get defensive very easily. I shouldn't have stormed off."

She noticed Omair break into a thoughtful grin. "Thank you, Ventura." Ventura smiled back at him. "You're very mesmerizing, you know."

She felt her face fluster from his comment. She then gave an awkward pat to the horse and motioned it forward. "Let's keep going." Ventura turned away in embarrassment, and Omair caught on.

"Are you blushing?" he teased her playfully.

"W-what? No!" Ventura protested. She pulled her hood over her head again to hide her flustering as she quickened her pace.

"I think you are, Ventura."

Ventura groaned. "That's not my real name."

Omair paused. "It's not? You're willing to tell me?"

Ventura sighed. "Well, if you're gonna tease me, I figured you might as well know." She took off her hood and looked at Omair. "It's Duna."

Omair got off his horse and extended his hand toward her. "It's nice to finally have met you, Duna." Duna giggled and took his hand in hers. "So...does this make us friends now?"

Duna thought for a moment. "I guess it does."

Omair grinned from ear to ear. "You're my very first friend." Duna realized that, technically, Omair was her first friend too.

She only smiled and continued on the path right next to Omair.

****

Throughout the day, Omair and Duna spent more time talking. Duna still remained cautious but was less defensive after confessing her name.

"So no one has called you Duna since your mother?"

She shook her head. "Yeah, it was such a long time ago." She tried to picture her mother's face without thinking of the fire. She thought back to before the incident when they were happy together. "I remember when I was younger, I dreamt of being a singer." Omair stared at her intently.

"Did you really?" Duna gave a gentle nod.

"I told my mom that I would travel across the land and overseas to perform for the whole world." As she told Omair, her eyes twinkled with more joy than he had ever seen from her before. "She believed I could, she believed that I could do anything I wanted to. I even wrote songs to sing." Though her smile soon faded. She looked down at the floor sadly. "She was my whole world. I wasn't ready to lose her or the others." She paused. "I wasn't ready to lose my family."

Omair saw the sadness in her eyes. He stood beside her and instinctively wiped the tear from her eye. Duna looked up, a bit startled, but he just calmly said, "What was your mother like?"

Duna looked away and thought. "My mother was loving. She believed there was good in everyone, no matter who they were." She smiled. "That's why she loved my father."

Omair listened quietly, then spoke again. "Was your father a vampire too?" Duna nodded. "My father was a vampire, but my mother was human." Omair couldn't help but show his surprise. Duna blushed as she realized what she just admitted. She confessed to being half-human.

Omair understood. "You lived with humans, didn't you?" Duna couldn't respond. She was speechless again.

She felt hot, like the flames that closed in on her in her mind. Her breaths got short, and she felt the flames closing in on her.

Omair rested his hand on her shoulder calmly. Duna looked up at him and had a sense of tranquility fall over her.

Not sure how Duna would react, Omair embraced her gently. Duna didn't push away. She let the tears fall on his shoulder. She hugged him back, but she didn't speak. They stood there in the vast space, holding on to one another silently.

After a few moments, Omair released her so they could keep walking. He didn't ask anything more about her past. Instead, he changed the topic of conversation. Omair spoke about how long he'd been an inquisitor and where he'd traveled to.

Duna chimed in and told him of all the places she'd seen. "I guess in one way or another, you did kind of live your dream of seeing the world, huh?"

She laughed. "I guess I did." Omair smiled to himself.

"That's what it's all about."

Duna looked up to see the path before them. "It is, Omair. It is."

Chapter 11

Duna and Omair arrived at Eugena by nightfall. The journey had been long and tedious, but they had both gained a friend from it.

When they saw the candlelights in the distance, they smiled at one another. Omair calmly pulled the horse and sheep behind him.

Omair started to tie up the animals near an inn when Duna started sniffing the air. Vito did too. "You smell 'em, chico?" Vito growled. Omair was confused for a moment then he realized what they were after.

"Wait, we should find a place to stay for the night. Let's get Giles tomorrow after the royal gathering." Though Duna and Vito were already following the smell. Omair sighed and followed them. He'd wanted to spend more time talking to Duna now that they'd become friends. He didn't realize how focused she was on finding Giles. Their noses led them to a pub in the middle of the town. They could all hear the commotion coming from inside. Omair was hesitant to enter, but Duna immediately did, and Vito went in right after.

Omair followed slowly, but once he entered, he caught sight of the nobles and hid under a nearby table. The group of men at the table looked at him like he was crazy, but they shrugged and assumed he was drunk like the rest of them.

The music was loud, and there was a bustle of people within the pub. Duna swiftly moved through the crowd. She grabbed her laudanum bottle to pour some in the nobles' drinks when they weren't looking, but Omair, down on his hands and knees, followed right behind her. As

Duna neared their table, Omair grabbed her arm and pulled her behind the stage where people prepared to perform.

Duna turned around to face Omair. "What are you doing? I could easily drug them and finish them outside once they're drunk enough."

Omair shook his head and, in a loud whisper, said, "No, you don't understand. I recognize those nobles; they know me as an inquisitor. If they see me, our cover is blown!"

Duna rolled her eyes. "Then you stay back and let me handle it."

Yet Omair grabbed her arm tightly. Duna glared at him before he said, "You can't go by them with your weapons on you; they'll notice. Please listen; they'll know something is wrong."

Duna wanted to argue but realized that Omair was right. She sighed and told Omair that she would think of a better plan. As she did, an older-looking fellow walked up to them both.

"What are you three doing back here? This is for performers only!" Duna tried to think of a good excuse to avoid causing a problem, but Vito and Omair were already ahead of her.

Omair pulled Duna close, and Vito stood in front of her to hide her visible weapons. "She's a new performer from out of town. She'll be singing tonight."

The man stared at Duna, who had a look of horror on her face. The man glared at Omair. "I don't buy it. She's not even dressed for it."

Omair scoffed. "Well, of course, she isn't, my good sir. As her agent, I have my lady dress for the occasion in her wardrobe. Every good performer knows not to arrive at a pub dressed for all to see. Shouldn't *you* know that?"

The man looked uncomfortable now. "Well, I never thought of it-"

"Of course, you didn't because you're not an artist like my lovely Shadow Dove here." Omair motioned toward petrified Duna, who was frozen in his arms.

The man nodded. "Okay, well, have her dressed soon. She's up next to perform." The man looked over at Vito. "Also, no pets allowed."

Before Omair could respond, Duna placed her hand over Vito's head. "Vito stays." Omair gave the man a nervous smile.

"I have to do what the Lady says." The man only rolled his eyes as he walked away.

Duna then shook Omair off of her. "¿Estás bromeando? I can't perform!"

Omair smiled lovingly. "Well, of course you can. I've heard you sing, and your voice is beautiful."

Duna flushed again. "I hum and whistle a tune occasionally, but I haven't sung in public in years, Omair!"

Omair just gently guided her towards the dressing room behind the stage by the hand. "You'll be fine. Besides," Omair pulled out a fitted black dress from the closet, "this dress will look perfect on you."

Duna flinched when she saw the dress. She hadn't shown off her curves in years, and to have to do that on stage was mortifying. Nevertheless, she grabbed the dress reluctantly for the sake of the mission. She went into an empty room to change quickly. Duna cringed at the tight fitting of the gown but walked out to meet Vito and Omair anyway. They both stared at her in awe. The gown fit her like a glove. It was tied at the waist, and the skirt covered her assassin boots beneath it. The dress opened at the top to expose her sepia-colored neck, and it tightened around her torso, giving her an hourglass figure.

"Well? How do I look?" she asked sheepishly.

Omair's face was the color of a tomato at this point. "You're breathtaking...." Duna stared at him as she turned a light shade of pink around her cheeks.

Only then the man returned to tell them that she was next in five minutes. Her bashfulness quickly turned into fear.

"I'm not ready!" Duna's breathing quickened, and she felt like fainting. "I can't do this. Everyone will be looking at me...what if I mess up?"

Omair grabbed her shoulders. "Hey, Duna, look at me." Her eyes met Omair's. "It's gonna be okay. Just breathe."

Duna calmed down a bit from his words. "Okay."

Omair looked around and caught sight of a piano. "What songs do you know?" Duna tried to think, but no songs came to mind. Though it seemed Vito knew one. He went back into the dressing room and came back with a small notebook in his mouth.

Duna saw him and tried to grab the book from him, "¡Vito, Dámelo!" Yet Vito ran around her to get to Omair, who looked at the paper.

He read it over. "Were you hiding this?" Duna's face reddened. "I didn't know you were a talented songwriter."

"It was private!"

Omair showed her the page. "Something this good needs to be shared." The man returned. "Two minutes!"

Duna's heart was racing. She could hear the man introducing her on stage. "Now presenting our newest lady, Shadow Dove!" The crowd applauded her, but she was frozen. Omair managed to pull Duna towards the stage and huddle with her one last time. "Listen, it's now or never. I'll play your song on the piano using the notes you wrote down, but you have to sing."

Duna looked at Omair nervously. "I'm scared."

Omair looked at Duna with all seriousness. "Duna, you are the most remarkable person I've ever met. You can do this. You can live your dream tonight; go be Shadow Dove." She nodded slowly and started to walk towards the stage.

When she stepped up there, she could feel all eyes watching her. All she could see was the light that was shining on her.

She couldn't see anything but darkness beyond the stage light, but she could hear whispers.

But then, near the stage, she heard Omair call out to her. "You got this, Shadow Dove!" She gave a weak smile, and he started to play. She grabbed her cross necklace tightly to her chest, asking her mother for strength.

Duna then took a deep breath and started to sing.

Chapter 12

Once I was as innocent as a bride dressed in white
Always dreaming but never seeing
But I can never escape the demons of the night

Duna looked at Omair for reassurance as he kept his eyes locked on hers. It gave her the strength to go on.

Yet I'm still haunted by this being
It haunts me in my sleep
Why can't I escape?

Duna closed her eyes to picture her mother and sang the song she wrote for her. *I know we sew what we reap*

Yet I'm left torn like a drape
I am forever trapped in this nightmare of a life
Scared and shaken in a fright

She slowly wrapped her arms around herself as she remembered the flames. She could hear the voices calling out to her from her memory.

But I can't escape the demons in the night
I stay haunted by this being
As it frightens me during sleep

Duna tightened her eyes and clenched her fists in a rage of desperation, as if she was singing an angry plea.

I wish they'd take me out with a knife
And then there I'd be, out like a light

Yet as Omair watched, he began to see the pain that Duna truly felt inside. He saw the innocent girl return, but only for a moment.

I wish I was free from this tormented place
So I can finally breathe again

Tears began to stream down her face, but she kept singing. She sang her pain. *But I will never escape the demons that haunt the night*
I stay tortured by this being
As it torments me in my sleep

Duna then opened her eyes to face the crowd. She could see them clearly now. She wasn't afraid anymore. She stared directly at Giles.

By killing me, there was nothing to gain
Forever hidden beneath my disguise
You will never see my pain
I will never again hear those very lies

She pointed at Giles within the crowd as she sang the last verse.

So here I stand like a bride dressed in white

As the crowd in the pub cheered for her performance, Duna saw Giles quickly get up to leave. So rather than stay there to enjoy their applause, she leaped off the stage to chase after him. Vito was close behind her with her sword in his jaws.

The older man tried to stop Duna from leaving, but Omair quickly stepped in front of him. "Thank you so much for letting Shadow Dove perform, but she has places to be. Bye now." Omair gave a small wave and then turned to leave. The man tried to grab Omair, but he was already running for the door with Duna's clothes and weapons in hand.

Once he reached the door, Duna had already caught up with Giles in a nearby alley. She slashed the back of his legs, causing him to fall face forward. Duna then leaped in front of Giles to tower over him. He tried to stand again, but Duna grabbed him by the collar and lifted him with one hand. She then slammed him into the nearest wall just in time for Omair to be turning the corner to meet them.

Omair stood at the end of the alley, frozen for a moment as he processed what Duna was doing. He continued to watch until Duna turned to him in agitation to say, "What are you doing? Preguntarle."

Omair nodded and walked up to Giles, "What do you know about the disappearances of Devontae's prisoners?"

Giles nervously looked at both of them. "I-I don't know anything! I only imprisoned some lowly citizens!"

Duna scowled at him and shoved him harder into the wall. "¡Mentiroso! He knows something. Make him talk, or I'll slit his throat!" Giles started shaking uncontrollably and began to sob.

"No! Please, no! I'll talk! I'll talk!"

Omair calmly stepped forward. "We're listening."

Giles looked at the both of them. "There's this creature...he goes by Vladimir. He has the prisoners. He wants them for some reason."

Omair's brows furrowed. "Why does he want the prisoners? Where is he taking them?"

"I don't know exactly why, but he demanded them from me and the other nobles. He threatened us."

Omair thought for a moment. "How did he threaten you exactly? What is Vladimir?"

Giles shook his head. "I don't know. The nobles call him a beast, but I don't know more than that."

Duna slammed him into the wall again. "¡Idiota! Don't lie to us!"

Giles started sweating and sobbing uncontrollably again. "That's all I know! I swear! Now please let me go..." he begged.

Duna turned to Omair. "Your call."

Omair stared at Giles. "Where is Vladimir now?"

Giles looked away nervously. Duna reacted by pinning further into the wall until it cracked. "¡Habla!" she demanded.

"Okay! Okay!" Giles sighed, knowing he was defeated. "He's in Venetia."

Omair tensed at hearing the name of his hometown, but he focused on the task at hand. "Who else was involved with the missing prisoners?"

Giles pointed to the pub. "Every noble in there took part in it." Duna looked at him, waiting for his say.

Omair looked at Giles one last time. "You know nothing else?" Giles shook his head. Omair sighed. "Alright, do it."

Duna nodded, then pulled out her dagger to slice Giles's throat.

Omair looked away to avoid watching Giles choke to death from his own blood. He didn't want to hear him any longer. Duna took the liberty of draining the remainder of the blood when Giles had stained enough of his clothing.

Once she finished, she let Omair know. "Now we can head to Venetia to find Vladimir and end this nightmare once and for all."

Omair stopped her. "What about those nobles in the pub? You could just drain their blood, and that would be the end of it."

Duna looked at Omair, puzzled. "I don't feel comfortable doing that without knowing their exact crimes. Also, this isn't over. We need to find this Vladimir person."

Omair looked away nervously. "Well, we could just end the case here. I mean, you got Giles like the princess wanted, and he already confessed to the missing prisoners. I could just send a letter to the princess and be finished."

Duna stared at Omair in disbelief. "You mean to tell me we've come all this way for nothing? What about the prisoners? What about justice? "

Omair didn't make eye contact. "Well...."

Duna shook her head. "You need to confirm that what Giles said is true. Besides, you made me perform in front of the whole pub. You're not flaking out on me now. We're going to Venetia."

Omair knew that Duna was right, so he agreed. "It's part of our deal."

Omair knew it was true, but deep down, he didn't want to return to his hometown. Omir had decided to put his past behind him, and he was hoping that it would stay there. So he focused on Duna.

Vito came out of the pub holding Duna's armor in his mouth. He dropped it at her feet. "Gracias, amigo." She said to him as she quickly changed out of the dress and into her armor once again. "Ah, that feels better."

Omair smiled, but his expression turned critical. "Duna?"

She looked up at him. "Hmm?" Omair hesitated for a bit to find the words.

"Your song... is there something you want to talk about?" Now Duna was the one to hesitate. Omair nodded. "It's okay. You don't have to tell me if you aren't ready to. Just know I'm here for you."

Duna gave him a weak smile. "Thank you." Vito chimed in with a bark, which caused both Duna and Omair to laugh.

"We should find a place to stay for the night."

Duna nodded in agreement. "Lead the way, Sir Inquisitor."

Omair chuckled. "Only if you follow, Lady Shadow Dove."

Chapter 13

Vito guided the sheep behind him with the ropes he held in his jaw. The trip to Venetia took them further away from Devontae, but Duna knew that it would be worth it. Omair had said that it would take two days to get there, but even though he wasn't happy about the destination, he enjoyed sharing the journey with Duna. She remembered that Venetia was his hometown and decided to ask Omair a bit about it. "So, any fond memories of your old place?"

Omair sighed. "I have a few, but they always bring up sullen feelings."

Duna nodded. "Do you want to go back?"

Duna noticed the troubled expression that Omair had. "Being completely honest, no." She stayed silent because she could relate.

Omair wasn't looking at her anymore. He hadn't spoken to his father in years. He could only imagine what he would say when he saw him again.

Omair imagined that he'd be disappointed in him for what he'd done with his life. His father was never one to help others because they hadn't helped him when his mother left. He didn't speak a word of this to Duna, though. Omair could only think silently to himself.

Eventually, Duna was the one to break the silence. "Where did you come up with the stage name Shadow Dove?"

Omair smiled to himself. "It was all I could think of at the moment. I also thought it suited you."

Duna eyed Omair curiously. "Do tell."

"I mean, as Ventura, you symbolize hope and devotion to the people, which is also what doves represent."

Duna nodded. "Go on."

"Doves symbolize a number of things. They can resemble innocence and purity but also stand for the Holy Spirit in religion. Doves can be navigators, deliver messages, and be gentle." Omair paused for a moment as his face reddened.

"I just thought a dove would be a good name since you are all of those things." Omair looked up at Duna with cherry cheeks. " You thank God before you eat and even before you kill, you find your way anywhere and survive on your own in the wilderness, but you're also kind and gentle to those who are innocent. Just like you were with that little girl in Devontae."

Duna had stopped walking to focus on him. "But most of all, you are a protector of peace and love. You fight even against yourself to keep others safe." Omair grabbed Duna's hand, which caused a feeling of butterflies in her stomach. "You have the divinity of an angel, yet the strength of a celestial warrior." Duna looked away sheepishly. "You are a shadow dove because you're a hero of the night."

Duna moved her hand away skittishly. "De acuerdo. I get your point. It was a good name."

Omair smiled. "And you're a great singer." Vito barked in agreement.

"Thanks, Chupie." Duna petted Vito and took the sheep from him so he could go chase a stick she threw for him.

Omair watched Vito run after the stick with a joyful grin. He took this time to speak to Duna alone. "So you mentioned that your mom was human?" Duna looked back at Omair, unsure of where he was going with his question. "If this is too personal, let me know. I just wanted to ask about the vampire thing."

Duna smirked. "Bueno. Go on."

"How does it work exactly? You being half-human."

Duna was confused. "Elaborate."

"I mean, you drink blood, but you can also ingest food. So do you need both food and blood to survive? Or could you just survive on blood alone? "

She thought for a moment. "Since I'm not technically dead, yes, I do need food to nourish the human part of me, but as a half-vampire, I don't drink as much blood as a normal vampire does. I can go days without blood, but if I have long blood withdrawals, my thirst for blood increases to the point where I start to lose control."

Omair stared intently. "Do you have your own blood?"

"Yes."

Omair's eyes widened. "So you can bleed out like a human?"

"Hypothetically speaking, yes. But I won't exactly *die*." She used air quotes to emphasize the *die* in her sentence. Omair stared at her, confused. "Listen, pure vampires can die from the sun, being stabbed in the heart, and being burned or drowned. They *can* die from things that can harm people, but because of their strength, speed, and resilience, it's very difficult to kill them."

Omair thought for a moment. "Wait, you said vampires can die from the sun. How come you can be out here in pure daylight?"

Duna took off her hood completely and showed Omair her arm. "I'm half-human. I need the sun, or else I wouldn't have color. I just wear the hood because of my job."

Omair stared Duna dead in the eye. "Can I ask something that's probably inappropriate?"

Duna shrugged. "Sure, why not?"

Omair inhaled sharply. "Do you get menstrual cycles as a half-vampire?"

Duna's face turned five shades of red. She looked away uncomfortably. "Uh...are you seriously asking me that?"

Omair nodded. "I won't make you answer if it's too much." Duna sighed. She knew that Omair meant well, but she'd never had to explain her half-vampire anatomy to anyone before.

"Okay, yes, I do. But the thing is, during my...*time*... I crave more blood than usual due to the loss of my own. Therefore, my blood withdrawals are more extreme."

Omair stared at Duna earnestly. "How riveting."

Duna could only stare at Omair with confusion. "You're weirder than most people, you know that?"

Omair nodded enthusiastically. "I do. Do other vampires like your blood?"

"Ew, no! ¡Qué asco! I'm still a vampire! My blood doesn't taste like a human's, it's not desirable." Omair nodded with full concentration.

Vito returned with the stick in his mouth. This time Omair was the one to grab it and throw it into the distance.

He didn't throw it as far as Duna had, but it was a decent distance to get Vito running. "Do you always throw sticks on your travels?"

"I do. Vito and I are always making things into a game. Even when we hunt, sometimes we split off so I can finish an assignment and he can catch a meal. Whoever gets back to our meeting place first wins."

Omair chuckled. "Must be nice to have a companion with you." Duna agreed. During the nights, sometimes, Duna would wake up in cold sweats as she dreamt of screams and burnings. Vito would cuddle next to her until she fell back asleep. Her panic attacks left her frozen in terror at night.

The one thing Duna hated more than anything was having to fall asleep. She was always afraid of waking up back in San Joaquin, seeing the ashes of her beloved pueblo. She didn't admit it to Omair, but Duna would kill for Vito. He was all she had left.

That animal was the only one who had stayed by her side through all these years. "So why were you at the Euryale Tavern anyway? It doesn't seem like you want to fraternize with anyone."

Duna laughed. "I keep a low profile, but I occasionally visit old companions."

"Isn't it dangerous to have friends as an assassin?"

Duna looked down to her feet. "It is; that's why I'm not close to anyone. To keep them safe from me. You have to trust people to have friends."

Omair glanced at Duna once more. "Do you trust me?" She was

silent for a moment. Omair stood there hoping she would say yes, hoping that he was more than just some travel partner.

"I don't trust anyone." Before Omair could respond, she put her hood up and began to lead the way, leaving him alone.

Chapter 14

Omair made a bit of conversation the rest of the way but didn't ask anything specific anymore. It bothered him a bit that, after everything, Duna didn't even trust him a little bit. He couldn't really be upset because she kept her distance, but they had agreed to be friends. He thought that meant something.

No matter how hard Omair tried, he couldn't shake the feeling off. His only friend turned out to be merely an acquaintance.

While Duna tried to justify her words, in her mind, she felt guilty for saying that to Omair.

Both of them were so lost in their own thoughts that neither of them could sense the tension they had created between them.

As Vito returned once more with the stick, he could instantly tell that something was wrong with them. So instead of giving either of them the stick, he walked up behind the horse and bit the back of her leg.

The horse let out a blood-curdling scream and stood on her hind legs in a panic. This caused Omair to lose control of the reins and fall forward. The horse, seeing how she wasn't being pulled anymore, bolted away from the group. Duna, not knowing what happened, chased after her.

Vito helped Omair stand on his feet as they watched Duna return with the four-legged beast. She handed the reins back to Omair silently and checked the back of the horse's hooves in case something had happened to her. When she was checking her back hooves, she noticed the large bite mark on her ankle.

Duna instantly glared at Vito, who hid behind Omair. "¡Vito, Hemos hablado de esto! If you're hungry, you can tell me! You're too old to be biting livestock!" Vito whimpered. "Don't you start crying; you know better! ¡No eres idiota!"

Omair gently patted Vito's head. "Maybe he was just playing."

Duna frowned at Omair. "Don't defend him."

Omair looked at the sky. "It looks to be the afternoon, it's about time to eat anyway." Duna gave a long sigh.

"Vito and I can go get an animal from the forest. The ovejas can be for dinner." Omair stared at her, confused. She quietly pointed to the sheep. "I want to avoid a panic." He nodded.

Duna whistled to Vito so he could follow her. As they walked, she spoke to him. "I know why you did that." Vito gave a low whine, pretending like he had no idea what she was referring to. "You can't just make a scene when you don't like something." Vito gave Duna a knowing look. "What's that look for? I do not make a scene!"

Vito shook his head. *You're in such denial.*

"Listen here, perro. I don't have to trust him, and you can't convince me otherwise." Vito groaned. *Siempre haces esto....*

Duna turned away from him angrily and sat down near a tree to look out for any animals. Vito walked up to her and rested his head on her thigh. She looked down at him. *Está bien confiar en alguien. It's okay to trust someone.*

Duna shook her head. "I can't do that with my line of work. ¿Qué tal si algo le pasa?"

Vito sat up and shook his head. *Nothing will happen. It's okay to have a friend.*

She looked back at Omair, who was standing by the horse. He was feeding him some carrots. She broke into a smile.

Vito licked her face, and Duna wrapped him in a hug. "Okay, maybe one friend will do."

Chapter 15

Duna and Vito returned with a wild boar. Omair didn't manage to hide his surprise. "How did you find it?"

"Vito smelled it; today's hunt was thanks to him." Omair patted Vito's head as a reward.

Duna set the boar down, and as she was about to make the fire, Omair tapped her shoulder. She turned and was greeted by a bouquet of colorful wildflowers. She met Omair's gaze with her countenance being the shade of a rose. "I know you may not trust me yet, but I promise to work towards gaining your trust every day, no matter how long it takes."

She silently looked at Omair, then the bouquet. Duna was so stunned in a fluster when Vito pushed her toward Omair, causing her to stumble. As she did, Omair caught her with one arm as the other held the blossoms. When she looked up, she could see that her face was only inches from his.

By now, Duna was in such a daze she wasn't sure how to speak. She wasn't sure what to do in this position. Part of her wanted to run away immediately, and another part of her wanted to stay in this timeless moment forever— but she was too busy processing what was happening to do either one.

Luckily, she was able to stand on her own after Omair gently helped her up. She brushed herself off and thanked him as she accepted the flowers awkwardly. Omair only smiled at her shyness and prepared to help her again. "I'll get the sticks for the fire." As he was leaving, Duna called out to him. He turned to her without a second thought.

Her embarrassment immediately returned, but she managed to utter the words, "I'll do my best to trust you someday." Omair gave her a warm smile. He appreciated how hard she was trying to open up, but she wasn't obligated to do that.

Omair responded by saying, "For now, being your friend is enough."

Now he was the one to leave her standing alone, contemplating her words as he left for supplies.

****

When Omair returned with the supplies, he saw Duna saving the flowers in her bag. "What are you doing?"

"Saving the flowers as a hierba for later."

"Most girls just keep them as decoration."

Duna stared at Omair. "Do I look like most girls?" She motioned to her swords and armor. Omair laughed.

"I suppose you don't. Most of them wear dresses."

She threw a dagger at Omair that barely missed his eye as he dodged it. "Hey, you could have hit me!" Duna gave a wicked grin.

"If I wanted to hit you, I would have. I need the maple from the tree behind you. I just used my dagger to make an incision in the tree."

Omair glowered at her. "You didn't throw the dagger just for that."

Duna smirked. "Also, to scare you."

Omair shivered. "You already do that without throwing knives at me, thank you." That made Duna blush.

"Aww, gracias rubio." Omair wanted to tell her that wasn't a compliment, but he didn't want to dodge another dagger, so he stayed quiet.

Vito came up beside Omair to help skin the boar. "Latinas are crazy," Omair whispered to him. Vito nodded. *Es cierto hermano.*

"Quit talking about me and get the maple, Omair."

Omair nodded obediently. "Yes, ma'am."

He used the dagger to continue carving the bark off of the tree to gather the maple in a leaf-like Duna had shown him. When he brought it to her, she gave her nod of approval, and they finished skinning the boar together.

Omair imagined that this was how married couples made food together. This must have been how his mother and father used to make food side by side. He couldn't help but steal a few glances at Duna every now and then. She looked radiant under the midday sun.

Even though she could feel Omair's eyes on her, she didn't look back. She tried to keep her focus on the task at hand instead of giving in to her emotions. Omair had tied the sheep and the horse to a nearby tree where Vito stood guard. Vito was also sent off to get supplies whenever they needed anything. Once the boar was prepared, Duna split the food evenly among them. Omair bit into the pork. "Mmmmm, this is delicious."

Duna smiled. "It's my mom's old recipe. We used to skin the animals in San Joaquin when I was little."

Omair listened as Duna explained to him how her village used to handle their livestock. As she did, Omair tried to think of where he had heard of the name before. He remembered his father vaguely mentioning it to him when he was younger.

Though he didn't mention it to Duna. He was just happy that she was finally talking about her mother without closing up again.

Chapter 16

The sun was slowly beginning to set on the horizon. Duna decided to choose a place to spend the night.

Omair was in charge of scouting the area to find a good place to put the animals. As he walked along the dirt in the darkness, he didn't notice how the path came to a sudden end. Before he could realize his mistake, he fell over the edge of the massive cliff, only being held up by the horse's reins.

He could see only darkness beneath him. Omair frantically held on to the horse's reigns. "D-Duna!" He cried.

As he did, the horse tried to back away from the edge to avoid falling, and in doing so, she managed to lift Omair a few feet up, but she wasn't strong enough to lift him completely. Vito was nearby and ran over to help lift Omair, but as he bit the reins, they broke. Omair's weight had made the reigns as frail as twine.

Omair cried out to Duna as he fell a hundred feet into a lake. Duna, hearing his scream, ran over to the cliff and soared into the water to pull him up.

"H-help!" he cried as he tried to maintain his head above water.

Duna grabbed his extended arm and carried him in her arms bridal style back over the cliff. He wrapped his arms around her neck as he shivered in the cool night air. "T-thank you," he stuttered, more cold than embarrassed.

"You're welcome, guero."

Duna set him down on the ground and helped him take off his

soaking shirt. When she did, she caught sight of whip marks all across Omair's back but just shook her head and placed her cloak around his cold body to dry him off gently. She then ordered Vito to bring more sticks to start a fire.

Within minutes, she had the fire started and began to make the food. Omair stared at his feet, ashamed that he had fallen while Duna prepared the food alone. She could visibly see his humiliation. "Hey, don't feel bad. You slipped, está bien." Omair didn't return her gaze. "Omair?"

"Yes...?"

"How did you get those whip marks on your back...?"

Omair sighed. "My father wouldn't let me leave the house without permission, and sometimes I would sneak out, so I was welcomed home by a beating anytime I did."

"I'm so sorry," she said to him.

"It's alright," he said with a smile. "I have you now, so I'm okay."

Duna blushed and sat down beside him. She grabbed a cloth and moved the cloak away from his face to clean off the remainder of the drops.

Omair watched her as she did. "Did your mother take care of you like this?"

Duna smiled. "It wasn't just her. My whole pueblo watched over me."

"What were they like?"

Duna thought about it as she moved the hair out of Omair's eyes. "They were simple and happy. We never needed anything more."

Omair watched Duna rinse the rag to use it once more, but before she could dab his face again, he grabbed her hand in his. Duna gawked at Omair for several seconds before he spoke. "Where are you going once this is over?"

She dropped the cloth and smiled clumsily. Duna lifted it off the ground, but Omair still had his eyes locked on hers. "I'll probably be off on my next assignment in another country."

Omair reached for Duna's hand again and held on to it firmly to prevent her from scurrying away again. "What if I went with you?"

Duna immediately turned her attention to the sheep. "¡Oh, mira eso! Food is ready!" Omair released her hands while she grabbed and cut the sheep meat.

Yet Omair wasn't letting her change the subject that easily. The moment she sat down, he asked again. "What if I left with you for your next job? I could help you a lot and spend time with you."

She didn't respond. "Vito, empieza a comer."

His impatience slowly grew. "Duna?" Silence. "Duna?" She didn't meet his eyes. Omair refused to be ignored by her any longer. He set his food aside and walked up to Duna until he was inches from her face.

Duna avoided his eyes, she could feel his warm breath on the back of her neck. When she still didn't look, he grabbed her gently by the chin and tilted her face up to look at him. "Well?" he said expectantly.

Her face flustered, and she immediately pushed him away. "I can't!" she said nervously. Omair looked a little hurt. Duna was facing him now. "Escucha, I travel alone. I prefer just to take Vito. It would be too complicated to bring anyone else."

Omair didn't sit back down, he stood beside her. "I don't want to lose contact with you if you leave."

She sighed. "I'm an assassin, it's better if you do."

Omair gasped. "Are you serious?" he asked in irritation. "That's not what friends do. They stick together no matter what!"

Duna looked at Omair, conflicted. "Omair, I understand, but look at us. You're an inquisitor. You can't risk your reputation by associating yourself with a killer. I'm a rebel hero fighting against the aristocracy while you're a part of it!"

"You know that's something that never mattered to me. I never saw you any differently."

Duna turned away. "I know Omair, but you can't come. We can stay friends, but you can't join my mission."

"You can't just keep pushing people away, Duna!" Now Vito looked up from his meal with his eyes widened. Omair continued. "I care about you. I will always be here, but you won't ever get to see that if you keep running from me."

Duna looked at him with tears welling in her eyes. "I'm trying to protect you and keep you safe."

Omair stepped closer to her. "I don't need to be kept safe."

Duna shook her head. "You're just a human, I don't want to hurt you." She started to back away, but Omair only stepped closer.

"Duna, please don't run." He extended his hand to her, but she didn't take it. When he saw that she wasn't coming any closer, he went over and pulled her into a hug. She shut her eyes, trying to keep from crying.

He kept his soaked arms around her body, almost as if he was trying to steal some of her warmth. So Duna allowed herself to lay her head against Omair's chest, even if it was just a moment.

"Duna, if anything, just promise me one thing."

"What?" She sniffed.

Omair gave a sad smile. "Even if I never get to see you again, just promise me that we'll always be friends." Duna stood there silently, thinking, "Duna, please promise."

Duna looked up at Omair, whose face was centimeters away from hers. She looked into his soulful eyes and caressed his face. "I promise, Omair."

Omair gave her a grateful smile. "I promise to always be there for you."

Duna stared at him. "And never lie?"

Omair nodded. "And never lie."

Duna smiled. "Then it's a promise between friends." Omair pulled her closer into the hug.

"So it is."

Chapter 17

As Omair began to completely dry, Duna taught him how to make a bed out of sticks and vines. She taught him what to look for, and he even started to get the hang of it. As she showed him, he stood over her, and every time he stood close enough, she expected to hear his heartbeat— but she never could.

Anytime Omair moved closer, he would quietly appreciate her beauty. There were moments when Omair tried to tie the sticks together using the vines that Duna grabbed his hands in hers to show him how to improve.

They laughed and gave each other sheepish smiles occasionally as they worked. As they did, Vito never hesitated to push Omair closer to Duna or vice versa. By the end of the night, they were used to being close to one another. When they finished, Duna started to settle in for the night before Omair said one more thing.

"Duna?" She turned to Omair. "Think about what I said. I'd be willing to follow you to the ends of the Earth if I had to." Duna only mustered a smile.

Omair then turned to rest, but Duna sat there watching him from afar, thinking of his offer.

****

Duna lay awake in her stick bed, staring up at the clouds. She couldn't sleep after what Omair had told her earlier. She opened her book again to write something, but she couldn't think of anything else to add.

Her thoughts were filled with Omair. So she sat up and saw that the fire had gone out, but she decided to leave it alone since the others had gone to sleep. Duna chose to go on a walk. She decided to leave her cloak and weapons behind. All she took was a single dagger.

The night was open and clear. She breathed in the fresh air. Her heart was a flutter, yet her mind was a mess. With each step she took, she felt her head and her heart at war with one another. Her heart wanted to run away with Omair and go explore the world with him for all eternity, but her head knew better than to jump into a commitment like that. Agreeing to take someone with her on her travels was more than a work relationship— it was a dedication.

So overall, she decided against taking Omair with her. It wasn't wise of her. Instead, she thought of writing letters to him and sending them by crow or maybe by dove. She gushed to herself within the darkness. The idea of sending letters back and forth sounded so enchanting to her. It was nothing that she'd ever done before.

Duna laughed to herself and twirled beneath the moonlight, and right under a tree, she caught sight of a single pale rose. She walked over to it and picked it up but cut her thumb on one of the thorns.

"Ow!" She looked down at her thumb and saw the blood spilling from it. Her blood covered the rose like a velvet cloth, which caused her to drop it.

Then within the darkness, she heard a familiar song. She froze and looked up to see that the grass around her had turned to dirt-covered ashes. Duna looked up, trying to find the moon, but was met with a blazing sky filled with smoke. She found herself falling short of breath as the song got louder and closer. The trees around her had disappeared now. All she could see was the burnt buildings of her past.

She heard distant voices and cries of pain that echoed in her mind. Tears began to pour from her eyes as she covered her ears.

"¡Basta! ¡Basta, ya!" she cried, but the screams only got louder, and the music was roaring in her ears. She could also just barely hear a soft yet threatening voice telling her, *Open your eyes.*

"No!" she yelled.

The voice got louder and more menacing. *Open your eyes, Duna.*

"¡No, basta! You can't make me look at you! You're not real!"

I am real, Duna. Now open your eyes.

Duna could feel her whole body shaking. "No!" she screamed, then without thinking, she reached for her knife and slashed the emptiness around her as she heard a scream. Duna sat up instantly, breathing hard. She was covered in sweat and had the dagger in her hand. She saw both Vito and Omair by her side. Omair was covering his face in shock.

"I-I'm sorry..." Duna cried. The tears came pouring before she could feel them burning down her cheeks. She expected Omair to scold her for slashing him, but he only took the knife gently and wrapped her in a hug.

Duna allowed herself to cry in Omair's arms. She sobbed so hard that her eyes burned. Vito stood by her side, licking her hand as a comfort. Omair rubbed her back gently. "It's okay, it's okay. I'm here."

Then, in that moment, Duna realized that whether or not she wanted to, she did trust Omair. She trusted him with this, with her secret. She trusted him to see her pain, to see her tears.

She embraced him tightly. She may not have been ready for a new travel companion, but she was ready for a friend. She was ready to not feel alone anymore. And when her hug tightened, so did Omair's. He wanted to prove that he wasn't afraid of whatever kept her up at night. He would do whatever he could to protect her from those demons, even if that meant holding her for the rest of the night.

Chapter 18

The next morning, Duna awoke in Omair's arms. She had fallen asleep next to him in her stick fort. Yet she didn't move away immediately; she stayed in his arms, rubbing the tiredness from her eyes. She felt safe with him and wanted to stay holding him for as long as she could. Unfortunately, she had to let him go when he awoke.

When he did, he looked at her with his tender eyes. Duna smiled quietly. "Morning, Dove," he teased her.

Duna giggled. "Morning, guero," she said as she gently poked his nose. Vito heard and jumped on top of both of them to give them morning kisses. They roared with laughter as they pushed Vito off the stick bed. Then they both looked at one another for a while silently.

No words were needed to know that they felt at peace for once. Both felt whole when the other was present. Almost like they didn't need anything else in the world anymore because they'd never be alone again.

Duna was the one to end the moment. "We should probably get ready to leave. We still have to get to Venetia."

Omair gave a gentle nod. "I'll help take everything down."

As Duna untied the branches and grabbed the horse, Omair cut some fruits from the tree like Duna had the first day they traveled together. She gave a small grin, which Vito saw. "¿Qué?" she asked when she caught Vito looking.

Vito smirked. *Mira, who's staring now?*

Duna rolled her eyes. "Deja de bromear, I'm not. I'm just..." Duna looked back at Omair, who was gathering herbs. She shook her head, "I'm just making sure everything's ready before we leave."

Omair walked over to Duna carrying some herbs and plants with him. He handed them to her. "Thought you could use some eucalyptus."

Duna took the plants and thanked Omair. She then handed him the reins of the horse. "Let's head out."

Yet as she turned away, Omair grabbed her hand. She stared at him, confused. "Maybe you should ride the horse this time. You may actually start liking them." Duna was going to refuse, but Omair was already lifting her onto the horse. She was the color crimson as Omair had his hands gripped on her waist. Though she was in a fluster, she didn't refuse his touch.

Once she was firmly on the horse, Omair handed her the reins. "Okay, don't be nervous; we'll take it slow to start."

Though Duna was already reining the horse. "¡Arre! ¡Arre!" she said as she gently patted the back of the horse. She began to trot on Duna's command, which shocked Omair. "You know how to ride?"

Duna smirked. "Just because I don't use horses doesn't mean I don't know how to ride them."

Omair simpered. "You're just full of surprises, aren't you, Ventura?"

She chuckled. "I am, rubio."

Vito followed behind them as he watched Duna ride circles around Omair.

****

As Duna rode the horse, they reached an open dirt area that was bare for miles on end.

She looked back at the forest of trees behind them. "We pass through here?" she asked Omair.

He nodded. "We just have to pass this empty patch of land, and we'll arrive at Venetia."

Duna nodded and continued riding. Yet as they continued on, she began to recognize the land they traveled. It seemed distant, but also somewhat familiar, though she felt uneasy in her stomach. She wasn't recalling any fond memories from the last time she had been here. Her palms grew sweaty, and her head felt light. If it hadn't been for the fact that she was on the horse, she would have surely fainted.

Omair noticed her uneasiness and asked if she was alright. "I-I'm fine. Just a bit dizzy."

He offered to take the reins of the horse for her to rest, and she agreed. She expected the feeling to go away when she gave him control, but her uneasiness grew. She looked around, trying to distract herself, but memories came flooding back to her.

She saw herself learning to ride on these plains. Duna could see herself farming with others. She saw the other children playing in the fields that existed long ago. Tears came to her eyes as she watched the neighborly woman bring out tamales for everyone to eat. She turned away from the memory, but when she looked in the opposite direction, she could see the church everyone attended on Sunday services.

Duna kept trying to look away to distract herself, but wherever she looked, she saw something that reminded her of the past. She saw a slaughterhouse where they would skin the animals to prepare the food. She saw her old home where she used to live.

Duna closed her eyes tightly, holding back the tears that burned her eyes. She knew this place. She recognized it all too well. She promised herself that she would never return to this cursed land. She vowed to never look back.

She tightly grabbed the cross necklace that was around her neck. She could clearly see the faces of everyone she had lost. She could see the villagers laughing and smiling with her. She remembered when they used to sing songs around the fire together in the evenings. Duna grabbed her stomach as she held back a cry of pain.

Omair immediately stopped the horse. "Duna, what's wrong?" he asked worriedly.

Duna shook her head violently. "No, I can't do this." The tears burned her cheeks. "I can't be here..."

Omair wasn't sure what to do. "Duna, what do you need? I'm here." He tried to reach for her to help her down, but she pushed his arms away, then jumped off the horse herself and ran into the empty field as fast as she could.

She tried to stop the memories from coming, but they just came stronger. As she opened her eyes, she came across more images from her past.

"¡Basta! ¡Basta ya!" she shouted as she covered her ears. "¡No quiero verlo! ¡No quiero recordar más!"

Yet the further she ran, the more she saw until she was so far that she collapsed from exhaustion. She looked down at the floor as the tears poured from her face. Duna closed her eyes tightly. "Por favor, no me dejes mamá. No te vayas....." She lay on the floor silently, sobbing for several moments in a fetal position before Omair finally caught up to her. Vito sniffed Duna's face and tried to lick her tears away, but she pushed him away. Omair sat down next to Duna and gently pulled her up to embrace her. She fell into him, sobbing uncontrollably.

"It's okay, I'm here."

Duna shook her head. "Los perdí... I lost them....It was all my fault...."

Omair shook his head. "No, it wasn't."

Duna looked up at him with angry tears falling from her eyes. "How would you know? You weren't even there when it happened!"

Omair nodded calmly. "I may not have been there, but I know you. I know you would have never hurt them." Duna dove into Omair's arms for a tighter hug. He gently rubbed her back. "Just tell me what happened."

Chapter 19

San Joaquin was a beautiful pueblo when I was young, I'd grown up with my mamá and without my padre. I never knew him. I only knew what my mamá told me about him and what the other rancheros would be willing to tell me.

My mamá told me that my father had been a lonely vampire lost to the night. He used to roam wealthy castles and seduce the fairest maidens at parties. They would become his victims of the night. They called him the Shadow Lover.

But on one lonely night, he was passing through the pueblo in the hope of catching a quick meal, but then he lay eyes on my mamá.

She told me she had been tending to the animals when she saw my father. She described him as a fair-skinned, tall gentleman with jet-black hair. He was charming, and she was simple yet beautiful.

He had asked to stay with her for the night, and she agreed, but as he tried to bite her neck while entering the house, my mamá turned and pressed her silver knife right at his heart, then gently placed a finger over his lips; my mother had smiled. Which caught him by surprise. My mamá told me that she had pushed my father away playfully. "You won't bite me that easily, vampiro. Siempre tengo un cuchillo."

This had stunned my father and intrigued him, so he chose to spend a night with her this once. But that night soon turned into a week, then a month, and then into a year, until they married one another.

The town hadn't known he was a vampire, my mom told me that he'd survived on the livestock of the pueblo during the night. The farmers would wake up in anger, thinking that a chupacabra had drained their animals during their slumber. But my parents would play along to keep my father's secret.

Though my mamá was a devout Catholic, she had a soft spot for outcasts like my father. She thought he was just misunderstood, and I think she was right.

During the short time they spent together, they had tried to conceive a child but never could. But they were happy together. Well, they were happy for a time.

My father soon came to realize that he wasn't cut out to be a dad. He had been so lost in his feelings for my mamá, he didn't stop to consider what it would mean to have a vampire child. So instead of telling my mamá, he left in the night, leaving only a small letter behind.

She found it the next morning and burst into tears. With that letter, my father had left the silver knife that she had used to stop him from biting her the first night they met. The pueblo was her comfort. She'd tried to return to her life as if everything was normal, but she was fatigued with what she thought was grief. But the madronas knew what it was.

They checked her womb, and sure enough, she was pregnant! The madronas predicted that I would be a healthy baby girl.

My mamá, in all her grief, found joy in the idea of having a child. She knew that I would never have a father, but that I would have many women to help look after me to replace that empty space.

The whole pueblo made sure to take care of my mamá during her pregnancy. They were all overjoyed to hear that the village would be gaining a new member of the familia. But what started out as a blessing soon turned into a tribulation, for my mamá began showing signs of vampirism.

It started out slow at first, with my mamá being near animals and humans. But soon, she realized that she was also beginning to crave blood like my father had. Her worry grew over time. She always thought that if I was a vampire, I would have my father to help guide me. But since he left, I was to grow up with these abilities alone.

She spent much of her time trying to satisfy her thirst for red fluids. She did this through spinach, tomatoes, and potatoes due to their metallic taste. It gave the illusion of blood because of the high levels of iron in them. Yet, despite her efforts, it wasn't enough to satisfy my taste. My mamá knew that I would crave blood when I left her womb, but she wasn't sure how to protect me from the farmers of the pueblo.

As a few months passed, my mamá began to thin due to the lack of blood, so the matronas fed her frijoles, tamales, fajitas, soups, pollo, bistec, really anything to help her stay plump and healthy. (Her words, not mine.)

My mamá found that the chicken and steak they cooked were dry, so every time they made her something out of meat, she always asked for it slightly less cooked each day to enjoy the savory taste of iron in them. At first, the madronas didn't think anything of it, but soon they began to notice how undercooked the meat was.

The village began to grow suspicious, especially when they saw that the animals weren't being drained anymore. They thought it had something to do with my father and wondered if I was anything but human.

My mamá explained that in order to confirm their suspicions, the madronas served her a chicken that was so undercooked it would make any normal mortal sick for weeks on end.

They left her alone with the plate, and my mamá, being grateful for the blood, devoured the pollo like it was nothing. When the midwives returned, they immediately alerted the Padre, who burst into the room holding a cross and a bible in his hands.

My mamá dropped her plate in surprise. She had looked up at them in dread.

"¡Llevas una hija del diablo, mujer! You carry a devil child, woman!" he shouted at her. But my mamá didn't flinch at his angry words as he continued to swear and say how damned she was for bringing my father into the village. But the madradonas intervened.

"Mija, you are not of sin, but your husband is. We're just worried about you. You hold a child that yearns for what is most sacred, sangre. Please understand that she cannot live. She is the embodiment of evil."

My mamá had told me that she had glared at them all with angry eyes. Tears welled up, but she didn't hesitate to respond. "No, my child is holy, ella es de dios. You're the ones who will be damned for murdering an infant."

They had tried to convince her otherwise, but my mamá sent them away.

Yet that didn't stop Padre Jose from threatening to finish me the moment I was born. "You won't get the chance, viejo," she spat.

He left, disappointed in what he had considered to be the most faithful catholic of the pueblo. My mamá sat there, holding her small belly. She wrapped her arms around me tightly. "No dejaré que te lastimen, mija. I'll protect you."

She had told me that when night fell, she was prepared to leave the village to start another life elsewhere. She had her horse and bags, ready to leave, but as she reached for the door, she felt water fall between her thighs.

What she had thought was water turned out to be blood oozing out of her womb. My mamá screamed at the top of her lungs as she tried to get a cloth to stop the bleeding, but the contractions stopped her from getting very far.

In minutes, the midwives entered her home and prepared for her bed rest. They lay out towels, prepped pillows on her back, and had a bucket of warm water ready to clean me the moment I arrived. My mamá wanted to argue and stop them, but all she could focus on was the pain she felt in her stomach.

The madronas slowly moved her towards the bed and had her lie down with her knees up and thighs spread. The women who weren't assisting the birth helped bring towels and lit plenty of candles for light. My mamá told me that a woman named Imelda had been the one to help deliver me. She was the one who told my mamá how to breathe and when to push.

What was supposed to have been a beautiful experience turned into a gruesome sight of horror. My mamá told me that when I did come, so much blood had left her body that the parteras wondered if she would survive.

But even within all the commotion, my mamá still had yet to hear me cry. The midwives had surrounded me to wrap me and check for breathing, but they fell into hushed whispers after a few seconds.

My mamá, still lying within her own fluids, asked, "¿Está respirando? Is she breathing?"

Imelda managed to stop the bleeding and went over to check on me. She had checked my breathing and looked up at my mamá and gave a sad shake of her head. My mamá's eyes had filled with burning tears. "¡No, no te creo! ¡Dámela!" Imelda slowly walked over to my mamá and handed me over.

I remember that every time my mamá would tell me this story, she would begin to cry all over again, just like she had that day.

She had embraced me tightly and cried out to God in pain. "¡Por favor, Dios, déjala vivir! ¡Quítame la vida Dios! ¡Tómalo! ¡Solo deja que mi bebé viva!"

The madronas around her stood there silently, watching my mamá crumble to pieces. She spent minutes crying out to God for what felt like hours. Eventually, one of the midwives suggested taking me away, but my mamá refused to let me go. And just as they were about to take me, my mamá heard me cry out.

"Sí, mija, llora. ¡Llora tu pequeño corazón!"

"La bebe vive!" shouted Imelda. The women around us gave shouts of praise to Dios. "¡Alabado sea el Señor!"

"¡Gracias a Dios!"

"¡Gloria a Dios!"

Padre Jose walked in, holding the cross around his neck. My mamá glared at him. "My baby is a gift from Dios, ella debe vivir. Si tratas de negarla, estarás negando a Dios mismo. If you deny her, you will be denying God himself."

He looked down at me, wrapped in the towels from the parteras. He slowly walked over to me, then took off his cross necklace and wrapped it around my neck. "Ella es de Dios. She is of God."

He then took a bow before my mamá and I, the other women, followed. "Protegeremos a esta niña en el nombre de Dios. We will protect this baby in the name of the Lord." My mamá had nodded. That was the moment the village had accepted me as one of their own.

The village decided to raise me with the values of a devout Catholic. I attended church and prayed like anyone else in town. They treated me like a human with special accommodations. For example, when I was hungry for blood, they washed a small rodent like a rat or farm animal for me to drink.

It was sweet, and on very few occasions when I behaved, I was allowed to feast on a pig, horse, and sometimes even a cow! But it didn't happen very often because the pueblo had to ration their animals.

So anytime I drained an animal, the village would cook the creature and serve it to me as meat. When it was a larger animal, the pueblo would gather together around a fire to feast in my honor. The whole village would celebrate by making up songs around the fire that we would sing together.

From a young age, I learned to hunt and skin the animals I had to eat with a machete. I was taught how to survive in the wilderness on longer hunts. I also learned how to cook and make food out of the natural elements of the forest.

I would attend church every Sunday, where Padre Jose would lead the sermons. I would sing along to the melodies they sang in the choir as they played the piano. I loved to watch their fingers dance across the keys as I listened to the rhythm of the song.

They never treated me any differently. If anything, they embraced my differences. Even when I hated myself for having to kill innocent critters, my mamá and Imelda would explain to me how I was sending the creatures to heaven with their other animal friends.

It made me feel less guilty for having to kill them. Every time I drained an animal, I was told to pray over my meal that God had granted me. Out of respect for the animal, I was required to thank it for its sacrifice, and we held funerals for every animal they buried. I survived on human foods during the day and blood during the night.

By the age of nine, I had started my period and began to crave more blood than usual. My mamá would cut the side of her arm and allow me to drink when livestock was low. But due to my excessive feeding needs, she couldn't satisfy my thirst. In response to this, the other rancheros offered their blood as a donation. Even Padre Jose let me drink his blood.

Not long after I turned nine, another vampire decided to visit our small pueblo. I saw him watching our village from a distance. At first, I thought he was a foreign visitor stopping by since travelers often stayed to rest here. But he was different. He didn't seem to have any intention of leaving.

I don't exactly remember how it happened, but after a few days of him stalking the town, I woke up one night to the sound of screaming. I sat up straight in my bed. I flew over to the window to see the commotion. I saw flames all around me. I could feel the heat against my skin, but I stayed there frozen. I watched as the people I'd known all my life ran for their lives. I saw them try to escape the beastly flames. Some were already dancing with the flames as they screamed in agony, but within those screams, I heard music.

Then I saw him. I saw the monster that had burned my town to shreds. Amongst the violence, he sat in the center of town, playing a depressing melody on a piano. He laughed menacingly as if he enjoyed the sounds of my people suffering.

I was about to fly over to attack him, but my mamá burst into my room. I turned to her frantically, "¡Mamá!" I called.

"¡Mija, tenemos que irnos ahora! We have to go now!" She grabbed my wrist tightly and pulled me through the house quickly. I followed close behind, almost tripping over my own feet as she dragged me. I noticed that she was still in her nightgown and only had a small bag over her shoulder.

When we reached the door, the strange man's arm burst through it with a strength I'd never seen in any human before. My mamá pushed me away from his grasp as he began to climb through. Then before I could react, she pulled out the knife my father left her from the bag and slashed the dagger over his left eye. He yelled like a demonio crawling out of the fiery depths of the infierno.

He hissed at my mamá, and I could clearly see the scar that the dagger had left on his left eye as his oozing black blood spilled out.

I was frozen until my mamá grabbed my wrist and pulled me towards the nearest window, where she told me to jump. I did as she said, then helped her climb through. When we did, she grabbed my hand and started running. We ran past my village that was burning away my memories of the past as I ran with her.

I expected my mamá to keep running with me when we reached the edge of the pueblo, but she stopped to hand me the bag. I looked down, confused, then back at her. "Go mija, go hide in the forest and don't stop running until you can't hear us anymore!"

But I didn't move. "Mamá no! I can't leave you and the others!" I tried to reach for her arm but she pushed me away.

"Mija, you have to leave now." Using the dagger, she sliced her wrist open.

"Mamá, stop! He'll smell you! " I grabbed her arm and tried to drink the blood, but she shoved me harder this time.

"¡Mija vete!"

I shook my head furiously as tears filled my eyes. "I won't leave without you, Mamá!" My mom turned to me angrily.

"¡Duna, vete ya! That's an order!" I stared at my mom, stunned; she'd never yelled at me like that before. "¡Vete ya!" she demanded. So I did. I ran deep into the woods where no one would find me. I didn't stop running 'til I lost all feeling in my legs and collapsed. I lay there under a tree until morning came. When I awoke, the sun was high overhead. I sat up and tiredly rubbed my eyes. I reached for the cross on my neck and was relieved to feel it there. I couldn't hear the screams anymore, but I knew I had to go back. I had to find my mamá.

So I cautiously made my way back to the pueblo. I moved at a quick pace but made sure that the vampire was nowhere to be found. When I caught my mamá's scent, I started sprinting towards the village. It hadn't mattered that she'd yelled at me because I was going to see her again!

But when I saw the village, I was met with nothing but ashes. My heart fell at the sight of ash and coal. My home was now nothing more than rubble that was left behind from a terrible tragedy. The tears started coming back, but I could still smell my mamá. I held on to

the little hope I had of maybe seeing her again. So I walked through the piles of black hills that were my town.

I searched for my friends and other people I knew, but saw no one. I was beginning to lose faith when I found my mamá's scent but saw no body. I froze for a moment. I could clearly smell her scent, but it was mixed with burnt sage. The tears welled up 'til I couldn't see clearly.

I looked around, hoping that I was wrong, hoping to see her again. Hoping to see anyone again. "Mamá?" I called.

I heard nothing.

"Mamá?" I called out again, but still nothing.

"¡Mamá!" I screamed out into the nothingness. Yet I heard no answer.

My world started to spin, and my legs felt numb. It was like I was stuck in a dream-like trance. I was living a nightmare that I couldn't wake up from.

"¡Mamá!" I yelled again, much louder this time. I took a step forward.

"Mamá, please, I need you!" But there was no one. I looked back at the pile of ashes and fell to the floor sobbing.

"¡Mamá no! Don't leave me here alone!" I lay on the floor with my legs to my chest. "¿Por que Dios? Why, God? Why?"

I lay there for what seemed like hours. I waited there in hopes that someone would find me, in hopes that someone would come up to me laughing, claiming that it was all some sick joke. But no one ever did.

When I realized that no one was coming, I sat up and saw that the only thing left standing was that damn piano. In a rage, I ran over to it and slammed my fists into it until the thing was unrecognizable. I stood over it, wanting nothing more than to kill the bastard who had taken my family.

But before I could do anything, an ashy breeze pushed against my hair blocking my vision. As I tried to move my hair out of my eyes in anger, I caught sight of the bag my mamá had given me; I finally went to open it. Inside were clothes, food, and the dagger she had used to stab him in a box. I turned towards the ashes of my mamá and collected the small pile into the box. I sealed it and placed it in the bag.

I looked back at the demolished piano. I knew from that moment on I would forever be alone.

Chapter 20

Omair stared at Duna as they sat in silence, but Duna didn't remain quiet very long. "Every single day since then, I've wished I were dead." Omair's eyes widened. Duna's fist tightened. "I've wished that I would have been the one to die instead of them!" The tears poured down her face once more. "I've wished that I would have saved them! I could have saved them! I was the only one with powers, and I couldn't even use them when I needed to!" She slammed her fists on the ground and made the ground shake beneath her, making Omair fall back.

"What was the point of surviving if it meant that I had to be all alone?!" she screamed. Omair tried to get near her, but her screams made him shy away. "I've tried to kill myself for years since losing them! I tried to burn myself with the same flames that took their lives....I tried drowning myself in a river....I even tried slicing my wrists in hopes of bleeding out entirely...but the wounds would heal every time...."

Duna sat there silently for a few moments while Omair sat down next to her again. "I did all of that so I could escape the lonely life I've had to live for 41 years....I lost them, and I blame myself every day for it...." She lowered her head to the ground as the tears came.

Omair didn't say anything, he only hugged her. Duna, too weak from tears to fight, gave into the embrace. He held her body close and tight, worried he'd lose her to this pain. He felt the tears from her eyes as he said, "I'm sorry...it was never your fault, Duna." She rested her head on his chest. "You were only a child, a child who was taken away from her only home."

Vito sat beside her with his head in her lap. Duna didn't respond. She wanted to believe him, but the guilt still taunted her.

"I won't let you hurt yourself again," Omair said. "I won't let you feel this anymore. I don't care what it takes to take your pain, but give it to me. Lean on me because I promise you I'm not going anywhere. I'm here."

Duna sniffed and pulled away from the hug. She gently wiped the last tears from her eyes. "Thank you." Omair nodded. Duna looked at Vito and petted his head. "I haven't hurt myself since I met Vito, but wanting to die never escapes my mind." She sighed. "Sometimes I wonder if having a mortal father would have been better. Besides, every human who finds out I'm a vampire thinks I'm going to hell anyway."

"Don't say that!" Duna looked at Omair, surprised. "That's anything but true! If anything, you're the one who's most likely to go to heaven!"

Duna shook her head. "I'm not. I kill people."

Omair moved closer to Duna and grabbed her hand in his. "You kill bad people, you save the good ones." Duna didn't seem convinced. "Listen, I'm not one to get religious, but I do know that God rewards those in good faith. You're like a guardian angel who banishes the evil of the world." Duna sat silently. "You do everything in the name of God. You would never hurt anyone who didn't deserve it, and that is the most honorable thing any vampire can do."

Duna stared at Omair. "Really?"

Omair nodded. "Really." He pulled her into another hug and kissed her forehead. Omair then cupped her face to face her. "Let's go."

Duna gave a weak nod and let Omair carry her toward the horse. He placed her on it as he pulled her away from San Joaquin.

Chapter 21

As they traveled on, Duna was silent, processing everything that had just happened. Omair didn't speak either. He remembered now why San Joaquin had sounded familiar. When he was young, legends of a vampire who burned a village down spread like wildfire.

Towns and kingdoms became cautious about monsters after what was known as *The Tragedy of San Joaquin.* It was said to have had no survivors except a single child who had escaped but was never found.

The fire had happened forty-one years ago, meaning that Duna was fifty. She had grown accustomed to being alone after losing her family, and when she tried to find other humans to accept her, they cast her away. Duna hung her head low. She thought back to her first human kill.

It was a few months after her village was born. She had been traveling from town to town in hopes of finding a new home. At first, the humans were kind to her and took pity, but when she started to crave blood, she learned the hard truth about vampires.

They immediately attacked her with fire and pitchforks in their hands. "Devil child!" they yelled. "Demon creature!" When the crowd started closing in on her, she ran as quickly as she could until their screams faded away. She hid in the woods alone, just like she did when she ran from her home.

At first, she thought that some towns weren't used to vampires, but when she tried to find comfort in another town, they sent her off with pitchforks once again. What she didn't know was that during that time, word was spreading across the land of what happened in San Joaquin. Villages and kingdoms were on high alert for any monsters at all.

So Duna started to prey on the livestock of animals from small villages. She would strike in the dead of night when most farmers were asleep. She was caught sometimes and left the village soon after. Most nights were spent in the woods alone or in abandoned buildings.

Duna started to realize that she was slowly becoming the vampire who had stalked her village. The more time she spent around villages, the more she craved human blood. She wasn't able to survive on the little animal blood she managed to drain. It was beginning to worry her— but seeing as she had no other choice, she continued hunting farm animals from villages.

That is, until the festival.

She had gone to visit Verona because of the many farmers living there, but when she arrived, she noticed the sounds of celebration. She knew she should leave, but her curiosity got the better of her, so she went to investigate. Duna saw townspeople singing and dancing in the streets. Children were running around with smiles on their faces. The feeling reminded her of pueblo before it died.

She gave a small frown when a young woman noticed her. She walked over to Duna, holding her children next to her. "Oh dear, are you alright?"

Duna was confused as to what she referred to until she looked down at her clothes. Her clothes had grown ragged over the past year. She didn't have the money to afford anything new. She just smiled at the woman politely. "No gracias, I'm fine."

The woman continued to stare at Duna. "Would you like to celebrate with my children and me?" Duna looked at her other two kids. They smiled and waved to her. She hadn't played with any other children in months. Part of her worried that they would discover what she was, but another part of her longed for the comfort of a family. So she agreed.

As the sun began to set, she spent the evening with the children and the mother. The mother never asked Duna where she came from, but she never took her eyes off of her. Duna couldn't care less; she was just happy to be a part of something again.

Though as time passed, Duna started to get hungry. When the mother noticed, she bought some food for her to eat. She accepted it politely but knew that the food couldn't satisfy her thirst for mortal blood.

She tried to ignore the feeling, but the longer she spent next to the children, the more she wanted to bite them.

Every time she got the urge to drink, she would bite her lip tightly and turn away from them. She had never taken blood from anyone forcefully. It was wrong, and she knew it.

At one point, she tried to leave the mother and her children to find animals to feast on but couldn't see any. Even if she could have seen any, the mother didn't let her leave her sight for even a moment. As her thirst grew, so did her cravings. No matter how much she tried, she couldn't control her instincts.

When one of the boys gave Duna a hug, her nose was filled with the smell of his scent, and without thinking, she started to reach for his neck. Before she did, the mother called her son to see something, and he released her. Then as if getting out of a trance, Duna snapped back to reality.

As she watched the boy return with his mother, tears slowly fell from her eyes. As much as she wanted to, she couldn't live among humans as one of their kind because, deep down, she would always be a vampire.

So before the mother could see her, she hid among the crowd of villagers and disappeared into the shadows. Duna moved to leave the town as quickly as possible, but humans met her at every corner. When they did, the urge to dig into their flesh grew, but she would cover her mouth and run in the opposite direction, only to be met by more humans.

They would notice her panic and ask if she was alright, but she didn't bother giving them a response. She just kept running. She ran and ran, trying to keep everyone else safe from her, but she was cornered into a back alley with humans at the end.

Duna grabbed her stomach as the pain of hunger consumed her. She imagined that this is what it felt like to be a zombie deprived of brains to devour.

She tried to avert her eyes from the people, but their smells would only grow stronger. She clawed the walls of the alley, feeling an unfamiliar sensation falling over her, like an ancient strength that vampires possessed.

It was moments like this she wished her father hadn't left her. Maybe if he had stayed, she wouldn't have had to suffer alone. Maybe he would have taught her what being a vampire truly meant instead of her having to learn alone.

As the feelings grew stronger, so did she, until she had to use her own nails to claw her arm down from attacking the people before her. She stumbled back into the shadows and found a window, which she burst through to find shelter from the crowd. When she landed inside, she was met with the old furniture and chairs of a small bedroom.

She sighed, grateful to finally be alone. Duna stood up to dust herself off, hoping to hide in there until it was safe to escape. Yet as she made her plans, she started to smell something. She froze as she noticed a presence standing behind her.

Duna slowly turned around to see an older gentleman standing at the doorway. She froze in fear; she could feel her claws extending. She felt her fangs growing sharper. She covered her mouth and turned away from the man as he drew closer. "¡No, Aléjate! Stay back!" she yelled as she pushed his arm away, in fear of what she might do to him.

Tears filled her eyes as the man grabbed her by the arm and pulled her towards him. She looked up at him and tried to push him away, but he tightened his grip. "You can't leave now. I've only had you for a minute," he said in a perverse tone.

Duna glared at him angrily. "¡Suelta me!" she demanded, but the man continued pulling her. While she wasn't afraid of what he would do, she was scared of hurting him until he placed his hand on her thigh.

As he did, Duna pulled his ear towards her and snapped his neck. Once she did, she held his limp body up with one hand to drain the remainder of his fluids dry. When finished, she dropped his body and took in a heavy breath.

She turned to the mirror and saw herself drenched in blood and sweat all over her clothes and mouth. She looked at herself in horror, she wanted to scream, but she heard footsteps behind her. "¡Ching, no manches!" she whispered to herself angrily. Duna turned around to see a woman holding a knife in her hands. She felt herself about to run again when the woman embraced her.

She stood there awkwardly, confused as she was covered with the man's blood. "You saved us," the woman whispered. Duna stared at her in bewilderment until she saw the three children who were standing behind the woman. "Children, go gather your things." The children disappeared into the darkness.

The woman turned back to Duna. "My husband was a terrible man who beat us and would even..." she looked down at Duna's torn bodice, "...force himself onto women."

Duna stared at the rip in her blouse. "Oh," she said.

The woman looked down at her husband. "He deserved to die. I was going to kill him myself tonight and escape during the festival. But then you came." She smiled at her gratefully. "You saved us."

Duna shook her head. "No, I'm no hero. I'm a monster." Tears filled her eyes as she shut them.

The woman shook her head. "No, dear, you're no monster." She grabbed Duna's face gently and kneeled down to meet her eyes. "A monster is someone who hurts those who are guiltless. A hero hurts those who are wicked. You get to decide how you want to use your ability, whether you target the innocent or evil." She looked down at her husband once more. She wiped the tears from her eyes. "You're no beast; you're our savior."

Duna gave a weak smile. "I'd rather be a savior than a monster."

The woman nodded. "Then choose to be one, my dear." She walked towards her desk, then pulled out a bag of coins. "Here, take this."

Duna grabbed the bag and saw the coins. "No, I couldn't," she protested, but the mother shook her head and pushed the bag towards her.

"I insist on paying you for your troubles. It's the least I could do." Duna accepted, and the children brought her new clothes for her to take to replace her old ones.

She looked around at the family gratefully. "Thank you," she said, in tears again.

"You deserve that and more," the woman said. "Now, let's leave before the others notice my husband's missing."

Duna followed the family through the village until they reached the end. "Come with us," the woman said.

Duna looked down at her things, then back at the family. She wanted to follow them with all her heart, but she knew that she would only burden them with her needs. "I'm sorry, but I can't."

The mother gave a gentle nod. "I understand." The family gave her one last hug. "Good luck."

As she watched them leave, Duna held on to the coins and bag of new clothing. She began to wonder what awaited her beyond this village without a family. She sighed, then turned away from the town as she trudged on alone.

This was the beginning of Ventura's journey.

Chapter 22

As they slowly made it out of the rough terrain, Duna looked back at the land she had once known. She held her cross close for a moment as Omair stopped to check on her. "You okay?" he asked.

Duna, without taking her eyes off the land, answered. "I am now."

"Can I ask one more thing before we go?" Duna nodded. "Whatever happened to your mother's ashes? I don't recall you saying anything about burying her."

Duna looked at the small bag. "That's cause I never did." Omair watched her quietly. "It all happened so quickly, I could never bring myself to bury her…at least I could never do it alone." She sighed. "I don't want to lose the only part of her I have left." Omair smiled. "I understand." He continued to pull her along for a while longer. "Did you have anyone after San Joaquin?"

Duna thought for a moment. For the longest time, she'd thought that before meeting Vito, she'd had no one— but now, looking back, she realized that wasn't entirely true at all. "I had Grant," she said as she thought back to their trip to Fabrizo.

"This cold cream is delicioso!" Duna exclaimed as she shoved the cone in her mouth. Grant had only smiled. "I knew you'd love it. It's called ice cream."

Duna looked down at her ice cream. "Well, then I love ice cream!"

Grant chuckled and wrapped an arm around Duna. "I knew you would, kid."

Duna smiled. "He took me to Fabrizo once for ice cream."

Omair smiled. "Sounds like he's a good friend."

Duna nodded. "He is."

Omair looked ahead in the distance. "We'll arrive at Venetia shortly." Duna looked down with a nod. "Until then," Omair picked a tulip from the ground and handed it to Duna, "I'm here to keep you company."

Duna accepted the flower with a sheepish smile. "I appreciate it, guerro."

Omair smiled. "Anything for you, Dove."

Vito barked at the both of them to let them know that they were nearing a village ahead. Duna was relieved that their journey was nearly over but also disappointed. She thought back to Omair's offer back in the forest. Once this was all over, what would become of their friendship?

As she thought to herself, the town before them became clearer in view. She could hear music and shouts of joy from the villagers. "What's that noise?" she asked.

Omair shook his head and groaned. "It's probably another stupid festival."

Duna gasped. "A festival?!"

Omair could see her eyes light up and immediately regretted insulting the fair. He sighed and smiled at her. "We can take a moment to celebrate with the others if you'd like."

Duna's face lit up like a child's. "¿En serio?" she asked. Omair gave her a puzzled smile. Duna blushed, realizing that Omair didn't understand Spanish. "Really?"

Omair chuckled. "Yes, really."

Duna squealed excitedly and took the reins of the horse. Omair, losing grasp of the reins, stumbled forward as she left him in the dust. Yet he only smiled at her excitement. Once Duna reached the town, she jumped off the horse and tied it to a nearby branch. Omair followed close behind.

Duna quietly observed the villagers from the corner of the street as they cheered and danced to ancient folk songs. She would gently clap her hands along with the music as she stood on the side.

He watched as her eyes danced with the rhythm of the music. Her eyes were wide, and for a moment, Omair could imagine how Duna was before the fire. For a second, it was like she was a little girl again with her family.

Part of her wanted to dance with them. When the song ended, Duna's eyes saddened. She looked down at her clothes and swords as if remembering who she was. She sighed. There was no way she could go out in the streets without looking suspicious. She pulled her hood further over her scalp.

Omair noticed and turned to Duna as another song began to play. Duna looked up at him, surprised, but he only smiled. "Dance with me?" Duna blushed and looked away awkwardly. "Don't tell me that you don't know how to dance now," he said with a knowing look.

"I haven't danced in forever."

Omair smiled. "C'mon, I saw the way you looked at them. You know you want to."

Duna shook her head gently with a laugh. "I'm not sure I remember how."

Omair extended his hand to her. She stared down at it, then up at him. "I'll remind you."

Duna looked down at Omair's hand again, then to Vito, who pushed her towards him. "Vale, vale, lo entiendo," she mumbled to Vito. She accepted Omair's hand and allowed herself to be guided toward the crowd.

Then Omair turned, grabbed both her hands, and began swaying side to side with the music. Duna moved with the rhythm as if they were both walking on water together. When the music quickened its pace, Omair twirled Duna around and drew her close. Duna flushed but continued moving with Omair. They spun together in a circular motion. While Duna looked to the others around them, Omair never took his gaze off of her. She looked back at Omair and smiled.

He then grabbed her by the hips and lifted her up in the air for a spin, and for a moment, Duna felt light as a feather in his arms. When she was in the air, she extended her arms out wide as if she was about to take flight.

Omair from below her was grinning as he twirled her into the air. Duna lifted her face like she was laughing with the sky. The breeze caused her hood to fall from her face to reveal her radiant glow beneath the sunlight, and it took Omair's breath away.

As he gently returned her back to the ground, her feet touched the floor ever so gently. In this moment, Omair saw her; he could finally see Duna for the first time. For once, he could see the *real* her smiling among the crowd.

When she stood again on her own two feet, she removed her cloak and weapons to set them next to Vito and returned to the crowd in a fit of giggles. Now she was the one to take Omair's hand and spin him around.

Omair, caught by surprise, lost his balance, and right before he fell, Duna grabbed his hand and pulled him towards her. When he finally regained his posture, he was inches from her face. He froze. Though Duna only laughed and gently poked his nose. "Oh, rubio," she said with a grin. She then proceeded to dance with a stranger who offered their hand.

The villagers were now switching partners, and Omair was left dancing with a much older woman. Though he had no complaints, he eyed Duna carefully. For the first time ever, Duna seemed genuinely happy and relaxed. She was finally free, at least for now.

Once again, the crowd switched partners, and Omair tried to reach for Duna but was taken away by another woman. Duna herself was whisked away by a younger gentleman. Then on the final turn, Omair managed to catch Duna once more before she could escape again. By then, the music had stopped as they both stood there, gazing into one another's eyes.

Part of Omair wanted to move in towards her to see what she would do. He wanted to hold her close but feared that it would make her uncomfortable. Duna, seeing his thoughts running wild, kissed his cheek gently. Omair, snapping back into reality, placed his hand over where she'd kissed him. "Thanks for the dance, guerro."

He wanted to return the favor, but just before he did, he heard a voice from behind him.

"Hello, Omair."

Chapter 23

Duna saw Omair's whole expression change when he heard those words. He slowly released her as the crowd continued their dance. He didn't turn around immediately. His face darkened as he said, "Hello, Father." Duna covered her mouth to hide her surprise.

Omair turned to face him. His father was a thick gentleman with a long gray beard. His eyes were crystal blue, like Omair's, and when they stood side by side, Duna could see the resemblance.

Neither one smiled. They stood there glaring at one another for several seconds before Duna stepped in. "Oh, hello, sir. It's so nice to meet you." She walked up to the older man and extended her hand in a warm greeting. "I'm a friend of Omair's."

Omair's father only scoffed and turned to his son. "What are you doing with a degenerate like her?"

Duna looked at the man, appalled by his statement. Before she could answer, Omair stepped in front of her like a shield. "Pay him no mind Duna, you shouldn't waste such good manners on a wrench like him."

His father tensed. "That's no way to speak to the man who raised you." Omair glowered. "And that's no way to speak to a lady."

Duna grabbed Omair's arm gently. "Omair, está bien. It's okay. I've heard worse."

He looked at Duna sternly. "No, Duna. It's not right. He should respect you like you deserve."

She flushed for a moment before grabbing his hand. "I know, but it's best not to make a scene in public. We still have a job to do."

Omair looked back at his father, then at the villagers dancing. He sighed. "You're right. Just let me talk to him alone for a bit." Duna gave a gentle nod, then called Vito over to follow her.

Omair returned his gaze to his father. "What do you want?"

His father snickered. "Relax, boy. Let's take a walk." Omair took one last look at Duna before agreeing. As they walked away from everyone, his father spoke again. "Been years since you last visited."

"Yes, and for good reason."

His father sighed. "I know."

Omair looked up at him. "I just have one thing to ask you." His father listened. "Why did you lie about Mom?"

His father looked away and brushed his hands through his beard. Omair could see the tears fill his eyes. "Your mother..." His father placed a hand on his shoulder. "Your mother was my world. When she left, she took all my dreams with her." His father covered his eyes with his other hand for a moment. He inhaled sharply to regain his composure. "When she left, I didn't want you to ever get hurt like I did. I didn't want anyone to take away that happy little boy I saw."

Omair pushed his hand away. "That's no reason to keep someone isolated from the world. I was alone for years, and when I tried to talk to other people, they turned me away because I had no social skills whatsoever." Omair's eyes filled with tears. He turned away from his father. "I get that Mom hurt you, but that doesn't mean it'll happen to me."

"How do you know? I saw the way you looked at that vampire girl. You think she'll accept you for what you are?" He looked at his father, surprised. "You didn't think I saw her fangs when she smiled?"

Omair tightened his fists. "What do you know about her? She's more than just that. She's the only person who's ever accepted me."

His father rolled his eyes. "You're just saying that because she hasn't tried to kill you yet. She's not family."

Omair glared at him. "How dare you say that about her! She's more family than you will ever be!" His father stood there stunned. Omair could see the pain in his eyes, but he didn't care. "How could you have kept me away from everyone? How could you have been so selfish as to deceive your own son?"

His father tried to answer. "I-I was trying to protect you..."

"Protect me? Protect me from what? The world or from Mom?" He stayed silent. "You never let me do anything, and when I tried to, you beat me to a pulp! You beat me so bad I couldn't even walk! I even have the marks on my back to prove it!" Omair lifted a bit of his shirt so his father could see the faded whip marks that made him shudder. "These marks are a reminder of what you did to me."

Omair's father's tears were streaming down his face. "I-I'm sorry...I was afraid I'd lose you too...." He looked to the ground. "But I guess I already have...."

Omair angrily wiped the tears from his eyes. "Just....don't come find me when I leave again, okay? I know you don't approve of my job or how I live my life, so it's better just to stay away." Omair said.

His father tried to reach for his arm, but he turned to walk away. "Oh, and one more thing." His father looked up at him. "Duna isn't a degenerate, she's a hero who goes by the name of Ventura." His father sighed. "You messed up a lot with me, Dad, but I won't let you disrespect her like that."

"If you really cared that much for her, you would let her go." Omair glared at him. "She's in danger as long as she's with you."

Omair snapped. "I can't believe that you have the audacity to tell me that! You don't think I'm trying to keep her safe?"

His father looked at him through angry tears. "I don't know, son. I thought you knew better than to bring those you care for in harm's way."

Omair scoffed. "You don't know what you're talking about."

"I may not have been the best role model, but I sure as hell know I raised you better than that."

Omair laughed. "You didn't raise me. You imprisoned me, and I will never forgive you for that." He turned away from him. "Don't plan on ever seeing me again because you won't." He then stormed off away from his father.

Chapter 24

Duna sat next to Vito on a stool near the dancing villagers when they both saw Omair walking towards them. Vito stood up and ran over to him, but Duna was more hesitant to approach him. Omair patted Vito gently and gave Duna a weak smile. She made her way towards him. "What happened?"

Omair sighed. "Nothing important, just family stuff." Duna didn't ask anything further and stayed quiet. Omair noticed her expression and stepped closer to her. "Hey, don't worry." He said as he caressed her face gently. "I'm okay."

Duna gently moved Omair's hand away from her face nervously. "I know that, it's just...he's your only family left."

Omair shook his head. "That's not true," He grabbed her hand in his. "You're my family now, too."

Duna's face flushed. "Um...."

Omair chuckled. "Don't worry, it's just a term of endearment. You don't have to do anything, you just mean a lot to me."

Duna smiled. "Thanks, Omair."

They spent the rest of the day at the festival in the town, enjoying the music and buying snacks.

Near the evening time, after dancing to the point of exhaustion, Duna sat on a small hill near Venetia next to Omair and Vito. They talked and laughed for a few hours as the sunset.

"So, how did you come up with the name Ventura anyway?"

Duna thought for a moment as she took another sip of her apple cider. "I came up with the name with Grant when I was thirteen. I was at the Euryale Tavern late one night, drinking grape juice with the others when we were joking around with names." Duna smiled at the memory.

"What about a name that means lucky?" Talon said, holding a bottle of rum in his hands.

"No, you need a name that will bring you good fortune!" chimed another monster. Duna thought to herself on the mini stool of the tavern.

"Maybe Felicity? It means luck and good fortune in Latin!" said Talon.

Duna shook her head. "Eso suena tonto. That sounds dumb," she said. Grant only smiled. "What do you think, Grant?" Duna asked him.

"I think you shouldn't pick Felicity." Duna giggled. "What about Faustina?"

Duna groaned. "Eww, no."

Grant snapped his fingers. "Oh, I got it!" Grant turned around and pulled out an old book and opened it to a page, then handed it to Duna. He pointed to a word on the page for her to read.

"Ventura?" she read, a bit confused.

Grant nodded. "It's a nickname of one of the characters. She's a thief who steals from the rich but gives to the poor."

Duna smiled. "It's perfect!" She jumped off her stool and soared over the tavern table. She had a hand on her hip and a dagger pointing to the sky. "From this day forward, I will be known as Ventura, the lucky assassin!"

The monsters of the tavern laughed and cheered in celebration. "I'll drink to that!" said Talon, as he raised his beer to her. Duna giggled as Grant patted her shoulder.

"You'll make a great Ventura, kid." Duna smiled.

She looked back at Omair. "The name was his idea, but I liked it so much that I decided to keep it."

Omair took a sip of his cider. "You must really care about Grant."

She nodded to herself. "He's kinda like family."

Omair placed a hand on her knee. "He sounds like good family."

She nodded. She looked down at her swords. When she was younger and decided to become an assassin, Grant had helped her forge her swords.

He had helped her draw out designs for it and planned it out. She had wanted a religious symbol on the sword to show that even though she would be killing, she would remain a holy servant of the Lord.

She remembered the first time she held her two swords in her hands. They had been so large that Grant had to help her hold them the first time.

"Do you like them?"

Duna nodded enthusiastically as she admired the wing-like design around the crosses. "I love it!" she said. Grant only smiled. "How did you even learn how to make swords?"

Grant kneeled down to sit beside Duna. "As a Cherufe, my family and I hid in the volcanoes of Chile away from the humans. But when humans tried to enter the volcano, my family and I had to flee. " He looked back at Duna. "Kind of like how you had to run away from your village."

Duna gave a sad nod of understanding. "Lo siento, Grant. I'm sorry."

But Grant just patted Duna on the head gently. "Eh, don't worry about it. Anyway, we had to learn to make a living amongst humans. So my father became a blacksmith and made weapons for knights and warriors of the land."

Duna stared at Grant in wonder. "¡Que padre!" she said with a grin. Grant smiled. "But how did you end up at the tavern?"

Grant looked down at her. "As much as I loved being a blacksmith with my father, I'd always wanted to open my own bar. So when I moved to Verona, I did just that." Duna smiled. "I'm glad you did."

"And why is that?"

Duna leaned on Grant's arm. "Because if you hadn't moved to Verona, I would've never met you."

Grant had chuckled and given Duna a tight embrace. "I'm glad I came too, kid."

Duna smiled to herself as she thought of him. "What's the smile for?" Omair asked. "Nothing, just reminiscing. But we should find a place to stay for the night. The moon's coming up."

Omair looked to the sky. "Or we can stay here a bit longer." He wrapped an arm around her shoulder.

Duna looked at the sky, then back at Omair. "Maybe just a moment longer," she said as she leaned into his chest to stare at the sky.

She pulled out her notebook to write a phrase, *The stars were like jewels in the sky.* Omair leaned over to look at her words. "What are you writing?"

Duna smiled. "Thinking of new song ideas." Omair chuckled.

"Let me write something." Duna handed him the pen and book. Omair took the pen and wrote, *But no jewel could ever match the beauty of the Shadow Dove.* He handed the book back to her.

Duna read the line and blushed. "Oh, guerro," she gushed.

Omair smiled. "You're beautiful, Duna."

She smiled. "Thanks Omair." She said as she lay her head against his chest once more.

Chapter 25

Duna woke up once again in Omair's grasp. She yawned and looked to the sky. She calculated that it was past 10 PM.

As she did, Omair groggily sat up beside her. "We should have found a room hours ago," she remarked.

Omair rubbed his eyes awake. "Sorry, but I couldn't miss an opportunity to sleep next to you again."

Duna sighed, then stood up to clean her clothes from the grass. "Where are we gonna rent a room at this hour?" she asked.

Omair chuckled. "I used to live here, remember? I'll find us a room."

Duna helped him to his feet. "You better; we still have to find Vladimir." Omair tensed when he heard her say that.

"Let's just find a room." Before she could comment further, he grabbed her hand and quickly pulled her towards a small inn within the village.

Duna was about to go in when she heard a faint musical melody. She turned away from Omair and Vito. "Do you hear that?"

Omair stared at Duna, confused. "Um...no?" He reached for her hand again. "We should really get a room to rest, though."

Duna pulled away again when she continued to hear the music. "Wait, I hear something." Duna walked towards the sound slowly, and Vito followed. Omair tried to pull Duna towards the inn, but she refused. "It's him."

Omair stared at her, perplexed. "Duna, you don't know that for sure," but she just ignored him. The tune acted as her guide, it sounded strangely familiar.

The melody led her away from the village near an abandoned building. As she neared closer, Vito stepped in front of her, growling at the building. "It's here," she whispered. She could hear the music getting louder as she neared closer.

Omair, fed up and uncomfortable, grabbed Duna by the shoulders to face him. She looked at him, like a spell had been broken. "Duna, stop!" She stared at Omair, lost. He hesitated. "Run away with me."

"¿Qué?"

Omair nodded desperately. "Yes, run away with me. We can leave this all behind. We can go somewhere new and start over! We don't need to find Vladimir. You've already given enough as Ventura! We can be happy together!"

Duna stared at Omair in disbelief. "Omair, how can you say that? We have a job to do. Why did we come all this way if we weren't going to finish?"

Omair nodded. "I know, I know, but that was before I realized how special you were to me." His father's words echoed in his ears. *She's in danger as long as she's with you.* Omair shook his head, refusing to let what his father said be true. "If you come with me, I'll keep you safe. I can protect you."

Duna shook her head. "No, Omair. We have to do this. Let's go in."

Omair shook her in desperation. "Duna, listen, you can't go; it's too dangerous!"

Duna pushed Omair off of her and drew her sword. "¿Que te pasa? What's gotten into you?"

Omair got down on his knees and held her hands tightly in a plea motion. "Please, Duna, let's leave."

She just shook her head and put her sword away. "No, Omair. If whatever's in there scares you, I'll face it alone. I came as a guardian to you, not as a distressed damsel." She then proceeded to kick the door down and walk in as Omair crawled to his feet to run after her. Vito tried to bite her cloak to hold her back, but she shooed him off and went on anyway.

As Duna entered, she waited to hear music, but it disappeared the moment she stepped foot in the building. She held her swords in both hands, unsure of what to expect. She could sense a presence but smelled nothing. Vladimir didn't seem like a mortal man. She saw Vito next to her. "Mantente cerca, Vito." He nodded as he kept his footsteps quiet.

Every step Duna took was met with the old creaking of an old building. It was the perfect hideout for a villain. It was dusty and occupied with a number of spiders. Omair stumbled into the building towards Duna. "Keep it down!" she whispered to him.

"We have to go."

Duna ignored his comment. "The music stopped. Something's wrong." She could feel herself tense as she continued walking.

Then the song started again, this time louder. Duna froze when she recognized the melody. Vito started growling beside her. Omair stood not far behind in confusion until he finally saw what they were looking at.

Under the moonlight sat a ghost-like gentleman with elongated fingers and claws that played at the keys of the piano. As he played, he flashed them a sinister smile. "Well, hello there, Ventura."

Chapter 26

Duna stared at the man before her. His skin was as pale as death itself, and his eyes were like diamond rubies.

He was dressed in formal attire like the wealthy nobles of the land, yet he had no scent like any mortal man she'd ever met. He was beautiful yet deceiving. Duna snapped out of her trance and held her swords in front of her.

"Vladimir," she spat. Vladimir only laughed.

"Nice to see that my reputation precedes me."

Duna glared at him. "Where are the prisoners, Vladimir?"

He stopped playing the keys and turned to Duna's hooded face. "What does it matter? They're all dead anyway."

Duna's heart dropped. She felt like she'd failed. She wasn't able to save the people. "Oh, don't look so down, Ventura," Vladimir said as he stood up from the instrument with a pout. "We all gotta die eventually, right?" He grinned.

Duna pointed her swords toward him. "Why did you do it, Vladimir?" she demanded.

"Please, call me Vlad. No need to be so formal all the time," he said as he adjusted his collar and coat. Duna continued scowling while Omair hid behind her. "But, if you must know...." He placed a single finger on the piano and scratched it across the top. "Demons get hungry too."

He flashed his fangs at her, and it made her gasp. "You're a vampire!"

"Unfortunately so, my dear, and your precious villagers were my meal." Duna stared in disbelief, she'd known vampires drained humans but not to this extent. "You....you monster..." she said, horrified.

Vlad gave a long sigh as he leaned on the piano and checked his nails. "Ah yes, that name is all too familiar."

Duna stepped forward. "How could you? A deed like that won't go unpunished!" She pointed her sword at him.

Vlad cackled. "Oh please, what are you? A saint?" He jumped down from the stage where the piano stood and calmly walked over to her until he was only a few feet away. "You're just as much of a killer as I am, sweetheart." Vladimir came closer. "Besides, I did those prisoners a favor. The nobles were just going to torture them anyway."

"It's not your place to make those kinds of decisions."

Vlad laughed. "Well, it is now! I went to those royals and nobles and gave them an offer they couldn't refuse!" Duna eyed Vlad expectantly. "I told them that they would either let me feast on the kingdom or I would drink them all dry like a prune." Vlad flashed his fangs once more. "So you see? It's all justified."

Duna angrily lunged at him with a sword to his throat, but Vlad easily moved away from her swing, causing Duna to fall on her knees. "Come now, I'm sure you can do better than that, Ventura," Vlad wickedly teased.

Duna stood up in seconds as Vlad flew at her and shoved her to the ground. She fell back, slamming into a wall that broke down to join the rest of the rubble of the building. Vlad gave a bored sigh. "Is this seriously the great Ventura I've heard so much about? I thought you'd be better than this. It's really rather disappointing," he said as he looked down at his claw-like fingernails.

Vito came to help Duna on her feet as she ran at Vlad once again, but this time when he moved, she swerved with him. He continued dodging her swings until she slashed his suit, causing a rip in the skin. When he stood up to examine it, Duna could see the black blood oozing out of his dead skin as it immediately repaired itself.

"Ah, so you can swing." He smiled. "This'll be fun." He ran towards her and clawed her arms and legs, causing her to fall from the pain. He turned around, expecting her to bleed out, but saw that her wounds closed immediately. He got a whiff of her strange scent as she stood up again with her swords ready. "You're no ordinary human, are you?" He smiled.

Duna, without answering, ran up the wall beside him and jumped off, preparing to stab his chest. Yet as she fell towards him, he moved aside, then grabbed her sword and threw her against the hard ground.

Omair ran over to her with her swords in his hands. Vito helped her up, but she pushed them both back. "Está bien, stay back, you two. You'll get hurt." She quickly grabbed her swords from Omair as she saw him approaching. Vlad, without as much hesitation, glided towards her and kicked her from behind. Duna was about to fall but caught herself.

Vlad watched her intently as she swung her swords at him. She missed each time, but he enjoyed the effort. He soared above her and pushed her, causing her to lose her balance. As she did, he caught sight of her fangs. Vlad clung to the wall above her and watched her growl and yell. *If she's a vampire, why doesn't she fight me like one?*

She turned around and jumped as she threw both swords at Vlad. He grinned and used his powers to change the direction of the swords to fly back toward her. Duna, in a panic, leaped away from both swords as they landed in front of her. "So pathetic," he laughed.

Duna snarled as she picked up her swords and flew towards him. Vlad held both swords back, then shoved her into a wall with both swords at her throat. She struggled to breathe as she saw Omair watching them.

She could see Omair's fearful expression. Duna looked away, she had to survive this; she couldn't let Omair see her die this way. She needed to keep him safe. She then kicked Vlad between the legs, causing him to fall to his knees. Duna fell to the ground, gasping for air. As she did, her hood fell from her face, revealing her raven locks. Vladimir stared at her with eyes wide.

"It's you...."

Chapter 27

Duna stared at him, confused. "W-what?" she said between tired breaths.

"You're the girl from the village." Duna froze as Vlad smiled. "Your eyes, I'd recognize those jewels anywhere."

Vlad stood up and made his way toward Duna. He picked up her sword and got on one knee. Vlad then proceeded to lift her chin with the sharp end of the sword as he drew his face near hers. "No wonder you're so weak...." Vlad looked down at Duna's necklace. "And you're religious?" Vlad looked at the cross with a grin. "Who ever heard of a religious vampire killer?"

Duna glared at him. "What's it to you?" she spat. Vlad only smiled.

"Just gives me a better understanding of who you are." Duna stared at Vlad in tired confusion. "What? Don't recognize me?"

He smirked, then dropped her chin and walked directly under the moonlight so she could see his face clearly. She lay there, gazing over his pale skin. She observed every detail of his face before her eyes found the scar. It was carved deep into his porcelain skin as a reminder of a failed killing.

She could feel her lungs closing up again and her heart pounding. "Y-you're...."

Vlad grinned at her realization. "Yes, I'm him." Duna flashed back to San Joaquin when he had tried to break into her house, and her mother cut him with the silver knife. "You see, silver doesn't usually leave any scars, but it seems like your mother blessed that knife long before I got there." He gently touched the scar, then grinned manically towards Duna.

Her nightmares replayed in her mind as she forced herself to stand again. Then Vlad, for the sake of fairness, tossed Duna her sword. She caught it in surprise, then stared at Vlad. "Don't act so surprised, deary. I want to break you at your best."

Duna's grip tightened around the handle of the sword. "I'm not afraid of you." Vlad laughed as her trembling hands wielded the sword before her.

"Who are you trying to fool? I know you fear me. You fear what I did all those years ago, don't you?" Duna sped towards him with both of her swords, but Vlad grabbed them both with his bare hands and shoved them back. Yet Duna didn't fall, setting both feet firmly on the ground. Vlad smiled. "You're no better than any of those measly little humans I burned that day."

Duna shook her head as she thought of her family from long ago. "That's not true!" she yelled as she took another stab at him.

Vlad swiftly moved away from the sword and kicked Duna in the stomach. She fell back but soared to the roof above Vladimir. "You really think you can hide up there?" Looking like a blur, Vlad flew up to Duna until he was face to face with her. "You're just praying that you forget what happened, don't you, Ventura?" Duna shook her head as Vlad drew closer. "Those mortals made you weak. I can make you strong, though," he said as he extended his hand towards her.

"No! Your tricks won't work on me!" she yelled as she threw her dagger at his chest as he caught it in his hand. He looked down at the knife. He laughed. "You tried to kill me with the same dagger your mother used." He gently held the weapon. "Such a sentiment." Duna pictured her mother handing her the bag before leaving her to the woods as he said those words.

Then with the same knife, Vlad flung it toward Duna's face. She moved quickly, but the knife caught her cloak, causing her to get stuck. "What? Can't move?" Duna then tugged at her cloak quickly as it ripped loudly. When she did, Vlad flew towards her.

Duna, not sure what to do, flew toward the ground away from him. "You can't escape this, Ventura!" he yelled as he used his abilities to pull her back from her cloak. Duna could feel the cloak tightening around her throat as he pulled. "You'll die a terrible death, just like your mother did!" She pictured her mother running back into the fire towards Vladimir. "You know..." he quipped, "the only reason your mother even ran back into San Joaquin was to protect you. She died...because of you."

Duna felt tears fill her eyes. "No....she.....didn't!" she yelled as untied her cloak from her neck.

Vladimir released her cloak and trudged towards her. Duna grabbed her neck as she gasped for air once more, but Vladimir pulled her up by her collar. Omair and Vito tried running toward him, but Vladimir used his powers to hold them in place.

"Despite what you may think, everyone in that town deserved to die."

Duna, barely able to breathe, shook her head. "N-no, they d-didn't. T-they were g-good."

Vlad gave a sad sigh. "You just don't get it, do you?" He slammed Duna into a wall as he tightened his grip around her neck. Duna tried to break free but felt herself losing consciousness. "Humans are weak! They don't deserve to live! The only thing they're good for is food! You would know that if you were a real vampire!"

Duna tried to move his hands from her neck but found it useless. So as she felt Vladimir's claws digging into her skin, she used her nails to slash his arm.

Vlad screeched in pain as he dropped Duna to the ground. She tried to reach for her swords, but Vladimir stomped over her hand. Duna bit down on her lip to keep her from screaming.

He was furious. "I can't believe you. You would go against your own kind just to help those pathetic mortals." He pressed his foot down harder on her hand. "They see you as a monster, just like me. If it wasn't for the fact that you pretended to be human, they would hate you just the same as me! Maybe worse!" Vlad lifted his foot from her hand as she sat up in pain.

As he watched her struggle, his expression softened. "You just don't understand how alike we really are, Ventura." He picked up her sword and examined it as he paced around her. "You hide what you really are just to be accepted in a society that doesn't want you." He then stabbed the ground with the sword so it could stand alone. "You try to be a noble warrior in a world that will never adore you for who you really are." He sighed and looked back at Duna. "I should know. I used to be like that. I tried to fit in with humans once."

Vlad circled Duna's crippled body. "I tried to be stronger than my thirst for blood." He stopped walking and looked at Omair and Vito. "But it was never enough...." Vlad turned back to Duna. "They cast me out into the shadows like the monster I was! They hated me just as they've hated you! I am not your enemy, Ventura. I am your friend." He paused to look at her. "I'm your friend." He leaned down and gently caressed Duna's face. "If I had gotten hold of you that night, I wouldn't have killed you, I would have raised you to be just like me."

Duna pulled her face away. "I would have never been like you!" she spat. Tears poured down her face. "My mamá showed me love and taught me the importance of integrity. My pueblo cared for me. They were my family, and you took them from me!" Duna shut her eyes as she tried to hide the tears.

Vlad rolled his eyes as he stood once more. "Oh, please! They never loved you! You were merely a pet to them, a circus act!" He looked back at her accusingly with his hair frazzled and crazed like the look in his eyes. "If the humans loved you so much, why didn't you find a new family, huh? Why didn't you find a new village to join? Why are you alone then, Ventura?"

Duna paused and looked down sadly. "Say it," he said with a harshness she'd only heard from strangers.

Duna refused to speak.

"Say it," he repeated.

Again she stayed silent.

"Say it!" he demanded.

"Because I'm a vampire!" she yelled.

Vlad nodded. "Exactly." He knelt down in front of Duna again. "But that's not your fault; you didn't choose this. Neither of us did. We've just dealt with the cards we were given." Duna looked up at Vlad with exhaustion.

"You don't have to be alone anymore. Join me. We can rule this land together. I drink twice as much as you manage to get in a week, Ventura. We could drink this kingdom to crisp if we wanted to. You'd never be hungry again."

Duna thought back to the countless nights of hunger before her patches. She thought of all the lonely nights she spent yearning for someone to hold and care for. She thought of the woman and her three children and how desperately she'd wanted to leave with them. She thought back to all those times she had resisted the urge to drink because it was wrong. She thought back to all the times that people had chased her out of villages. Yes, as a vampire, she was hated.

"The world will always hate you, so we might as well destroy it while we still can." As a vampire, Duna was feared, but she was also loved. She pictured Grant letting her be in the inn after hours when she had nowhere else to go. She thought of Taylor and how he had given her the first cloak she'd ever worn. She thought back to Vito spending countless nights by her side during her panic attacks. She thought of Omair, who was her only friend. She saw her mother holding her in her arms, comforting her when she cried. Vlad looked at her, eager to hear her accept.

"No," she said.

Vlad blinked in surprise. "Excuse me?"

Duna got on her knees in an attempt to stand. "No."

Vlad stood up in disbelief. "Why?" he demanded.

Duna stood on her own two feet as she answered. "I may be feared as a vampire, but I am loved as Ventura. People do care for me because of *who* I am." Vlad scowled. "People have loved me all of my life, and I refuse to become the monster that people have believed me to be for years. I am a hero. I am Ventura, and I will never stop fighting for those who cannot fight for themselves." Vlad tightened his fist. "And no matter what you say or do, my answer will always be no."

Chapter 28

Vlad gave a disappointed sigh. "You're wrong to refuse my offer, Ventura, but I guess you'll just have to live to suffer the consequences." He used his levitation to lift Duna off the ground and threw her into another wall.

"No!" Omair yelled as he ran towards Duna.

As she lay in the rubble of the walls, she weakly tried to push Omair away as he tried to pick her up. "Omair, get out of here. You'll get hurt."

Omair just turned to Vladimir angrily. "Vladimir, enough! I think she gets the point. Stop this!"

Duna stared at Omair, confused. "What are you doing?" she demanded. Vlad gave another flashing grin. "Oh, does she still not know? Awww, what a sweet surprise it must be for her! Why don't you explain it to her, Omair? Tell her what's really going on here." He smirked.

Duna looked up at Omair from the ground. "Omair, what is he talking about?" Omair sighed and looked away from her. "Omair?" she asked again.

He didn't meet her eyes as he responded. "I-I'm working with Vladimir."

Duna's heart fell. "¿Q-qué?"

Omair turned to Duna. "It wasn't supposed to be this way, I was trying to get you away from here so you'd be safe."

Duna was shaking her head. "¡No, no te creo! I don't believe you!" she yelled as she pushed Omair away.

"Wait, Duna. I can explain," he said as he grabbed her arms.

"No! I trusted you!" she yelled as the tears flooded her eyes. "I believed in you!"

Omair looked at her with a hurt look in his eyes. "I know. I'm sorry, Duna."

"¡No, suéltame!" she yelled as she jerked away from Omair and stood up angrily with a newfound rage. Duna glared at Vladimir as she walked over to pick the sword from the ground. "¡Terminemos esto! Let's finish this!"

Vlad smiled. "Gladly." He ran over to her as Duna held him back with her one sword. She managed to push him off while Vito ran to retrieve her other sword. "Gracias, Vito," she said before she ran towards Vladimir again.

Though, this time, instead of dodging her swings, Vlad grabbed both swords and pushed them towards Duna's throat. She tried to keep the swords at a distance, but as Vlad closed in on her, she saw that she was losing her grip on them. As Vlad kept pushing, he managed to shove her into a corner against a wall.

As he hovered over her, Duna's life flashed before her eyes. She saw her family, her friends, and even Omair. She saw her happiest moments and her saddest, all ones that she would miss.

Yet right as Duna was about to accept her fate, Vlad gave a cry of pain as she heard growls coming from his ankle. Vito had latched onto Vladimir's leg in an attempt to help Duna. As she heard Vlad struggling, a small smile formed on her face until Vlad was fed up with Vito.

"Damn dog!" he yelled as he kicked Vito all the way to the other side of the room, as he slammed into a wall. It wasn't enough to break through, but Vito landed on the ground, unconscious.

"¡Vito!" Duna screamed, but her cry was cut off by Vlad, who pushed her swords harder against her skin.

"This is the end, Ventura. You'll die a defeated hero, just like you were meant to." Duna tried to wriggle away in an attempt to help Vito, but it was no use. Vlad overpowered her strength easily. His abilities surpassed hers. He was a true vampire, while she was only a half-breed.

As the blades closed in, Duna caught a glimpse of Omair walking towards Vito with what looked like a dagger.

The burning fire came to mind as she saw everyone she loved be swallowed by the fire. She then looked at Vlad, who couldn't hide his look of surprise at her newfound determination.

"Get. off. Of. My. ¡Perro!" she yelled as she kicked Vladimir off of her and soared over to Vito.

Duna threw her sword towards Omair, who barely managed to dodge her swing before she grabbed Vito and her weapons. She then flew out the nearest hole in the wall, away from Venetia.

Chapter 29

They flew across the night sky as the moonlight lit their path. She didn't stop flying until she was certain she was miles away from them. She didn't land until she saw an empty church in the clearing.

Duna gently landed on a green patch of land in front of the building. With a heavy heart, she walked in there. holding Vito tightly in her arms. She opened the door gently in hopes of not waking anyone who was inside.

To her luck, the church Father found her entering the building. She tensed at the fear of what he might say to her. The last thing she needed was for another human to turn her away right now.

Yet to her surprise, the Father ran over to her chupacabra with a concerned look in his eyes. "Come, bring him to the altar," he ushered. Duna, relieved, obeyed and lay Vito down on the newly carpeted floor. The Father looked over his wounds. "He's badly injured," he said worriedly.

Duna sniffed. "Yeah…." She then pulled out her small bag with ointments and herbs she'd collected.

The Father watched silently as she cleaned Vito's wounds. Vito would wince, but Duna rubbed his back gently each time he did to assure him that everything was alright. "Oye, está bien, Vito. Estoy aquí, te tengo." He looked at her and closed his eyes as she continued.

The Father went to the back to bring back a wet cloth for her to use for the wounds. "Thank you," she said. He nodded as she took the rag. He watched her intently and looked down to see her tattered hair.

As he did, he noticed her dented armor and bloodied swords dripping from her side.

He stayed silent for a while as Duna cleaned Vito. He then observed what he thought was a dog until he saw the small spikes coming out of his back. The Father gave a sigh. *Oh, Lord, who have you called me to pray for today?* he thought to himself as he looked at the cross above the altar. He looked back to Duna and Vito. "What happened to you two?"

Duna stopped rubbing the ointment to think about her response. "I- we....got into some trouble back in Venetia." She didn't meet the Father's eyes.

He gave a gentle nod, then rested his hand over Duna's. She looked up at him. "May I pray over him?" Duna looked down at Vito, then nodded.

The Father took Duna's hand and placed them over Vito's body with his as they both bowed their heads to pray. "Lord, I ask that you heal this creature of all his injuries. I pray that your angels will surround this girl and her animal companion and give them blessings to light their path. I ask the Lord that you give this girl the serenity and the strength to continue on her path, whatever you have planned for her. Please be her guide through this difficult time, whatever it is she's going through...."

Duna felt her eyes water, but she held the tears in. The Father, hearing her sniff, placed his hand over her shoulder. "I pray that you let her continue fighting in your name, Jesus. Give them the healing they both need. Amen."

"Amen," she repeated. She looked up once again as she allowed herself to shed a single tear.

The Father smiled as he wiped away the tear with his finger. "God will heal you, my child."

Duna smiled. "I hope he can."

"All things can be done through Christ the Lord."

Duna chuckled. "Can the Lord fix something that's already been broken for so long?"

The Father stood up and sat down on a nearby seat. He patted the area next to him. "Come, sit." Duna looked at Vito. "He will be fine. Just let him rest for now." Duna listened and walked over to the Father and sat beside him. "Why do you feel broken?"

Duna looked down at her hands. "I've tried to live as well as possible, given my situation. But no matter how hard I try, nothing ever gets better. I've lost everything. My family, my only friend, and now...." Duna looked at Vito. "I'm on the verge of losing my pet...." Duna put her head in her hands. "Yet I did nothing wrong! I did nothing to deserve this!"

The Father patted her back gently. "I see. Do you know the story of Joseph and his brothers?"

Duna sniffed and nodded. "Yes."

"In that story, Joseph did nothing wrong, but he was his father's favorite. Because of this, his brothers were jealous and sold him into slavery. As a slave, he worked well and hard and was eventually recognized by the Pharaoh and given special responsibilities."

Duna thought back to the story. "I remember."

"I'm sure you also remember that while Joseph followed the Pharaoh's orders, he was imprisoned for a lie the Pharaoh's wife told him. So he was punished yet again."

"That wasn't fair at all."

The Father nodded. "You're right, it wasn't. But God gave Joseph a special gift, the ability to decipher dreams. God had a plan for Joseph, so while Joseph spent years rotting in prison, he held on for the promise of God. Then one day, the Pharaoh called for Joseph again after realizing his mistake and appointed him as one of his officials." Duna listened quietly.

"The point is..." He placed his hand on her shoulder again. "God had a plan for Joseph. He showed Joseph that even within a terrible storm, God was with him through it all." Duna looked up at the cross.

"People may leave you when you need them most, but God has never abandoned you. He will be your guide. He will be your light through the darkness." He looked down at her necklace. "But I think you already knew that, didn't you?"

Duna gave a sheepish smile. "I guess I just needed to be reminded of

God's plan." The Father nodded. "I understand." He stood. "Feel free to spend the night for you both to rest. There's food that I'll have prepared in the morning if you stay for breakfast." Duna nodded.

"Breakfast would be lovely, thank you." The Father nodded, then left Duna alone with herself and her thoughts for the rest of the night.

****

Duna tossed and turned in her sleep but couldn't bring herself to rest. She sat up, then opened her bag to try writing some more but was met with the last phrase Omair had written.

But no jewel could ever match the beauty of the Shadow Dove.

Duna angrily closed the book and threw it at the wall. Vito looked up from his resting place. Duna shook her head with tears in her eyes. "I'm sorry, Vito." She buried her head in her hands in a sob. "I can't believe I was so stupid for trusting him!" She whispered.

Vito wearily made his way over to Duna and rested his head on her leg. Duna sighed and gave Vito a weak smile.

"You don't need to limp on over here, Chupie," she said as she patted his head. She looked at the cross again. "God's gonna take us far away from me here, Vito. We won't need anyone else where we're going."

Vito didn't answer. He had already fallen asleep. Duna smiled and lay him down on the floor so she could cuddle up next to him to try to sleep herself.

Chapter 30

As the sun shone through the stained glass windows, Duna opened her eyes. She had fallen asleep next to Vito on the floor.

The Father had given her a blanket while she had been asleep during the night. She smiled and wrapped Vito in the blanket.

He tiredly looked over at her, then returned to sleep. Duna knew that she would have to get Vito an animal to drain after the night they'd both had.

Milton Keynes UK
Ingram Content Group UK Ltd.
UKHW020931201123
432908UK00022B/3446